Praise for Blake

"Ah, to be young in America—nothing matters and everything matters. And yet through the pervasive nihilism and irony, Blake Middleton finds a truth radiating with terrifying love and a radical self-acceptance. "I looked at myself in the mirror just now," he writes. "I just thought, this is what I am. Whatever I am. And that's okay.""

—Andrew James Weatherhead, author of *Todd*

"Takes you back to that not-so-long-ago time when the world was only threatening to go to Hell."

—Ben Loory, author of *Tales of Falling and Flying*

"*College Novel* uses clear language to describe unclear times. It's a spare examination of our relationships with popular culture and with each other."

—Timothy Willis Sanders, author of *Matt Meets Vik*

"I've never gone to college but I have lived in a college town long enough to probably know what it's like, and Blake Middleton's *College Novel*, which reads like a millennial adaptation of an early Richard Linklater film, perfectly captures the shitty essence of shitty sex, shitty drugs, and shitty punk rock house parties where the shitty keg quickly gets tapped and shitty garbage is used to keep the shitty backyard bonfire going till dawn. Two shitty thumbs up."

—Brian Alan Ellis, author of *Sad Laughter*

COLLEGE
NOVEL

COLLEGE NOVEL

BLAKE MIDDLETON

APOCALYPSE PARTY

APOCALYPSE PARTY

www.apocalypse-party.com

ISBN: 978-1-7335694-1-5

Copyright © 2019 by Blake Middleton

Cover design copyright © 2019 Matthew Revert

All rights reserved. No part of this book may be reproduced or transmitted in any form or by any means, electronic or mechanical, including photocopying, recording, or by any information storage and retrieval system, without the written consent of the publisher, except where permitted by law.

Printed in the USA.

For Johnny Kiosk

Jordan and Eric sat at a picnic table outside the library of a college in Jacksonville, Florida, where they were both seniors. 'I wanna die at Six Flags,' Jordan said.

'Six Flags is the funnest place to die,' Eric said. 'Or maybe the saddest.'

'What about Vegas?'

'Dying in Vegas seems too easy. I wanna die in Carson City.'

'I wanna die in North Korea.'

'Die by sneaking into North Korea,' Eric said. 'What's it called? The 38th parallel? The 38th lateral?'

'I'm gonna be a border guard in North Korea.'

'I'm almost positive you have to be North Korean.'

'I'm gonna choose whatever career I'm most likely to die from the quickest,' Jordan said. 'Wanna get drunk tonight?'

'I'm sick. The doctor said my nodes are fucked.'

'Drink a Cisco. You'll feel better.'

'Fuck off.'

Olivia walked up to the table. She sat down next to Jordan.

'What's up?' Eric said. 'How's the library?'

'It's okay.' She opened her purse, pulled out a pack of cigarettes.

'Didn't you buy that pack yesterday?' Eric said.

'Aubrey kept bumming them last night.'

'She did that to me the other day,' Eric said. 'I came home with like, four cigarettes.'

'Why wasn't I there?' Olivia said.

'I don't know. Aubrey wanted me to come over and talk about unionizing.'

'Unionizing Chicken Grill?' Jordan said.

Eric said yeah. 'I don't know why she thought I would want to start a union.' He looked down at his shirt. 'I wonder what this yellow shit on my shirt is.' He picked at it. 'Mustard.'

'Just drink one Cisco,' Jordan said. 'It's not going to kill you.'

Eric told Jordan to fuck off. No one said anything for a minute.

Jordan looked at Eric. 'Robert moved out of my storage closet,' he said.

'Shit,' Eric said. 'Where's he living now?'

'His parent's house.'

'Why?'

'He's too depressed to live in a closet.'

'I thought he was doing better.'

'He's fucked.'

'That's sad,' Olivia said.

'He's not making enough at Winn-Dixie to afford the closet. I told him he could work with me at the restaurant and make two-hundred a week, but he likes it at home, I guess. He drinks beer by the pool and hangs out with his golden retrievers. I think if Zach renews the lease I'm gonna live in the closet for a hundred a month.'

'I don't think the landlord is going to let that happen,' Eric said.

'That's what I'm thinking. She's already trying to evict us.'

'Zach is very good at making landlords hate him,' Eric said.

'He invited a ten-person folk-punk band over to do cocaine and play banjo on a Monday night. She gave us a seven-day notice to either shut up or get out.'

'Live in the dorms like me,' Olivia said.

'They're too expensive.'

'I think you're the only one that still lives in a dorm,' Eric said. 'Except Shithead.'

'Who's Shithead?'

'Matt,' Eric said. 'Tall and skinny. He was playing the drums at Aubrey's last party.'

'Wait…he has a mole like, near his lip.'

Eric said yeah.

'I made an asshole of myself one time when he came to one of the parties. He was like, making moves on my friend and I didn't realize it and he was going to go back to her apartment with her. I was like, drunk, and just kept saying, *really*, and he was just like, *yeah*.'

'Does that nine-eleven girl still come over?' Jordan asked Eric.

'Sam cut it off.' Sam was Eric's roommate. 'I still have her fancy vodka glass though.'

'Who's nine-eleven girl?' Olivia said.

'We were getting drunk on nine-eleven and being loud on Eric's balcony,' Jordan said. 'She asked us if we were celebrating nine-eleven and we said no and that we were just getting drunk not related to nine-eleven and she came up and drank with us. I feel like I get drunk on nine-eleven every year.'

'You're a patriot,' Olivia said.

Eric looked at Olivia. 'You look so morose,' he said.

'I'm very tired.'

'Meth,' Eric said. 'Do you need meth?'

'Do I need meth?'

'You should try meth. My supervisor tried to turn me onto meth the other day.'

'Michelle?'

'No. Michelle is insane.'

'She was strange to me when I was buying nachos,' Jordan said. 'She just kept telling me that she valued me as a person even though no else did. And then she made fun of me for wanting corn on my nachos.'

'She has a mole like, on the back of her neck that I'm afraid to ask about.'

'You shouldn't ask people about moles,' Olivia said. 'Okay. I need to go back in the library. Are you guys coming to my party Friday?'

Eric said yeah.

Olivia said cool. She said bye.

Eric and Jordan said bye. Olivia walked away.

'I don't know if I should tell my girlfriend that I have tonsillitis and she's probably going to have it soon,' Eric said. 'Her diet is so shitty her body isn't going to put up a fight. She eats toast and pizza. It's like, a touchy thing with her. I eat like shit but I get a fair amount of vegetables.'

'I eat fruit when I have money. I need to start stealing from Walmart again.'

'I remember when you were in there for so long and I was in the parking lot in one-hundred-degree weather going through minor withdrawals and then you stole a twenty-four of Coors and we got drunk again.' Eric looked at his phone. 'Fuck. I have to go to work.'

'I'll walk with you,' Jordan said. They stood and walked down a shady path toward the student union food court.

'I hope I don't die of something stupid like

tonsillitis,' Eric said.

'Die of a Peach Cisco overdose,' Jordan said.

'I'm not getting drunk tonight,' Eric said. 'I wanna die of a disease no one's had in like, a hundred and fifty years.'

'I wanna die while I'm young,' Jordan said. 'I don't wanna die while I'm old and shitty and stupid.'

'I wanna die of SARS. No, I wanna die of bird flu.'

'We could die in Reno,' Jordan said, and noticed a group of about a dozen people doing acroyoga on a bright green patch of grass outside the medical sciences building.

'I wanna die jerking off in lot 18,' Eric said, referring to the parking lot furthest away from campus. 'Like, they catch me and the cops come over and I just shoot myself in the head. I wanna be J.G. Ballard when I grow up. I liked *Crash* a lot.'

'I've heard a lot of white boys talk about *High Rise*. They always talk about how badass the opening is. Him eating his dog. White boys are fucking stupid.'

'I'm fucking stupid,' Eric said.

*

The next day Jordan sat in his film analysis class and watched *Inception*. Ten minutes into the movie Jordan left class. He walked around campus. He sat at a picnic table outside the freshman dorms. The weather was nice. It was late October, 2015. Jordan was surrounded by pine trees. There was a small pond nearby with some ducks in it. Robert walked up and sat across from Jordan.

'Fuck me,' Robert said.

'What's wrong?'

'Nothing.'

'Are you going to Olivia's party tomorrow?'

'I hate parties.'

'What else are you gonna do?'

'Nothing. I'm coming. I work at Winn-Dixie until ten though.'

'I wish Olivia would come by with a joint so I can get stoned and watch *Inception*.'

'Is that what you're watching?'

Jordan said yeah. 'I felt bored and left. I walked around and thought about freshman year. It's nice over here.'

'How's Winn-Dixie?' Jordan said.

'Love of my life.'

'You missed your chance to work with me. We hired some guy named Bobby that worked at a Chili's for ten years but doesn't know what a Cobb salad is.'

'I don't know what a Cobb salad is.'

'But he worked at Chili's for ten years.'

'What is a Cobb salad?'

'It's just a salad with eggs and avocado and bacon and shit.'

'That sounds good,' Robert said. 'Fuck. I want one of those.'

'He worked at Longhorn, Outback, and Chili's.'

'What a life,' Robert said. 'I feel like all those places have Cobb salads.'

Jordan said yeah. Neither of them said anything for a minute.

'Can you return things to a different store than where you bought it at?' Robert said.

'Sometimes.'

'I bought something at Walmart and want to return it to a different Walmart.'

'You can do that, I think. What do you wanna return?'

'A PlayStation time card.'

'How much was it?'

'Twenty bucks. I need money so I can buy food.'

'Buy a case of beer and bring it to Olivia's party.'

'I need to quit drinking so much,' Robert said. 'I'm gonna get sober and eat Cobb salads all day. I really want a Cobb salad right now.'

'I really wanna cop a salad right now,' Jordan said. 'I really want to kill a cop. Look at this guy.'

Jordan and Robert looked at an obese man skateboarding.

'That would be a heavy fall,' Robert said.

Jordan looked at other people walking. 'What do these people want from life?'

'I don't know. That's what I wanna know.'

'What does this person want from life?'

Robert stood. 'I'm going to sit by you so I can people-watch without looking insane.' He moved to Jordan's side of the table. Someone talking on a cell phone walked past Jordan and Robert. 'This is horrible marketing,' the person yelled.

'Did he just yell *horrible marketing*?' Robert said.

Jordan said yeah. 'Imagine getting upset over horrible marketing.'

'I feel like Jesus on the cross,' Robert said. 'Where can I get a nice Cobb salad?'

'Do you want a Cobb salad?' Jordan said. 'I can buy you a Cobb salad.'

'I don't need your Cobb salad hand-out. I'll buy a Cobby when I return my PlayStation bullshit.'

*

The next day Jordan walked inside Eric's apartment without knocking. He saw Eric's roommate, Sam, lying on the carpet shirtless, holding a beer.

'What's up?' Jordan said.

'Drinking beer on the floor,' Sam said. He stood and sat on the couch, turned on the PlayStation and the TV.

Jordan walked into the kitchen. Eric was staring into the fridge. 'Do I want the champagne of beers or the king of beers?'

'Champagne of beers,' Jordan said. 'Grab me one, too.' Eric handed Jordan a beer.

Jordan walked into the living room and sat on the couch next to Sam. Eric sat on a different couch. Sam was holding a controller, searching YouTube. He played 'Sound System' by Operation Ivy, and they talked and drank beer.

*

An hour later Jordan was shirtless on the back porch, sitting in a lawn chair, holding a beer. Sam was behind Jordan, digging through a bag of haircutting clippers. He attached one to a razor and ran it down the center of Jordan's head.

'Hell yeah,' Eric said. 'I'm pulling up a seat.' He grabbed a milk-crate and sat on top of it. 'Did you tell Emma you're shaving your head?' Emma was Jordan's girlfriend. They lived together with Zach, had been dating for about four years.

He texted Emma and said he was shaving his head.

Sam shaved off a long strip of Jordan's hair. 'That feels good,' Jordan said.

'Give me your shirt,' Eric said. 'It's going in the freezer.'

Jordan picked up his shirt and handed it to Eric, and Eric walked inside. He walked outside, drank some beer and burped. 'We'll be drunk by nine,' he said.

'Right when we have to drive,' Sam said.

'Perfect,' Eric said.

Sam finished shaving Jordan's head. Jordan rubbed his head. 'Does it look alright?'

'Looks good,' Eric said. 'Go ahead and pull your shirt out of the freezer.'

Jordan walked into the bathroom and looked in the mirror, rubbed his head with his hands. He walked into the kitchen and grabbed his shirt out of the freezer and put on the shirt.

'It's cold,' Jordan said.

'Feels nice, right?' Eric said.

'Not bad,' Jordan said.

'Every time I get drunk I put my shirt in the freezer before I fall asleep, and when I wake up, I make myself some hash browns with cheese and onions and put on my frozen shirt.'

They walked into the living room and sat on couches.

Sam talked about getting high at church when he was in high school.

Eric played the music video for the song 'Jesus is a friend of mine' by Sonseed.

Jordan said it sounded like the Talking Heads.

Sam said something about the guitar player's hip motions.

'I need more beer,' Eric said a few minutes later, then looked at Jordan. 'Wanna run up to the gas station?'

*

Eric opened his car door. 'Don't get in yet,' he said. He

pounded on the seat. 'I've got a minor cockroach infestation. You gotta pound the seat and they go back into hiding.'

Jordan pounded on the passenger seat. He saw a roach crawl under it.

On their way to the gas station, they passed a McDonald's, a Wendy's, a Taco Bell, a Walmart, another McDonald's.

Eric parked the car. 'Jesus is a friend of mine,' he said. 'He taught me how to praise my God and still play rock-n-roll. Man, I really wish they made eight-packs of tall-boys.' He opened the car door and walked inside the gas station. He walked outside the gas station, holding two four-packs of tall-boys. He got in the car. He looked at Jordan and held the four-packs next to each other. 'Eight-pack,' he said.

They drove back to Eric's apartment and walked inside.

Jordan looked at a large pill bottle on the counter. 'Let's take some 800 milligram ibuprofen and get fucked up,' Jordan said without thinking.

'Ibuprofen is generic trash,' Sam said. He was lying on the carpet again. He had a shirt on now. 'I only get high off Advil extra-strength.'

Eric put beer in the fridge. 'How does it feel to be two of the dumbest assholes on the world?' he said. He grabbed a beer and closed the fridge.

'Feels pretty good from down here,' Sam said. He took a drink of beer, spilt some on his face.

'You spilt beer on your face,' Eric said.

'That's what the carpet is for,' Sam said. He rolled over and rubbed his face on the carpet.

'Jesus Christ,' Eric said. 'I'm getting drunk tonight.' He pulled his shirt off, walked to the kitchen, put the shirt in the freezer.

*

A little later Eric's girlfriend, Kim, walked through the door. She sat on the couch next to Eric, put her feet over his legs.

'Can we get high tonight?' Jordan said to Kim a few minutes later.

Kim reached under the coffee table and pulled out a small bong.

'You're not allowed to smoke weed,' Sam said. 'You just got a haircut. That's illegal.'

Eric played depressing music on YouTube.

'Sounds like American Football,' Jordan said, and smoked marijuana.

'No,' Eric said.

'Very similar,' Sam said.

'Very sad,' Kim said.

'Sounds like Postal Service and American Football,' Jordan said.

'I'm gonna kill you,' Eric said.

Jordan handed the bong to Kim and Kim smoked marijuana.

'My mom is going to find out,' Sam said. 'This is smart. This is really smart.'

Kim handed Sam marijuana and Sam smoked marijuana.

'Play Ricky Calloway,' Jordan said.

'Shit,' Eric said. He played the song 'Get it Right' by Ricky Calloway. 'This is the guy that pressure washes UNF.'

UNF stands for University of North Florida. Jordan and his friends went there because you didn't have to write an essay to get accepted.

'What?' Kim said.

'This is Ricky fucking Calloway,' Eric said. 'He's a funk-singing pressure washer.'

'Shit,' Kim said.

'He's not good at pressure washing,' Sam said.

'Leave Ricky alone,' Eric said. 'He does a fantastic job of pressure washing. He's an excellent pressure washer and a magnificent funk-singer.'

'Yes he is,' Jordan said.

'I'm an asshole,' Sam said.

'You are,' Jordan said. 'He does a fantastic job.'

Jordan stood and walked into the kitchen. He opened the fridge and grabbed a beer. He opened a cabinet and picked up a glass. 'Why does this glass have Dough Mahoney written on it?'

'That's mine,' Eric said.

'Who's Dough Mahoney?'

'That's me. Dough Mahoney is my PEN name. I have to use a PEN name because I'm going to be the fucking president. Kim made me that.'

'Dough Mahoney,' Jordan said, and poured the beer into the glass.

'Dough Mahoney,' Eric said.

It was quiet for a few seconds. 'My mom is autistic,' Sam said.

'My Mom is Zach Braff and so am I,' Eric said. 'She's big Zach Braff and I'm little Zach Braff.'

'Shut up,' Sam said.

*

At Olivia's party an hour later Jordan sat around a table with Eric, Aubrey, Olivia, and Sam. It was a glass-top table and the base was made of ceramic dolphins. There was a large bong in the center of the table. Aubrey was painting something on a small canvas. In the living room there was a drum set, a guitar, a bass guitar, and a microphone. Jordan was stoned and staring at the ceramic dolphins, not really thinking about anything except how stoned he was. He heard a tambourine, looked up and saw Olivia smiling. It was her birthday. She was twenty-two.

'This is my tambourine,' she said, and shook it again.

'Cool.'

'I'm putting on Die Antwoord,' she said, and put on Die Antwoord. 'I want champagne.' She walked into the kitchen and came back with a bottle of cheap champagne and two glasses. She shook her tambourine. 'Would you like some?'

Jordan said sure.

She poured Jordan a glass of champagne, and he drank some.

'Don't drink before we toast,' Olivia said.

Jordan said sorry. He held up his glass and toasted with Olivia. Olivia smiled and then Jordan smiled.

'Where's Emma?' Olivia said.

'She didn't wanna come. She's probably at home watching *The Office*.'

Olivia shook the tambourine again. 'This isn't loud enough,' she said. 'I'm tired of hearing everyone's voice that hasn't said *hi* to me yet.'

Jordan didn't know what to say. He took another drink.

Someone walked up to Olivia and said happy birthday. The person was wearing a colorful jacket and eating a carrot. 'That jacket is funky fresh,' Sam said. 'That is some serious jazz.'

'Yeah man,' the carrot-guy said, and took a bite of his carrot and walked away.

'That was strange,' Jordan said.

'What?' Sam said.

'That whole thing,' Jordan said. 'What you just said.'

'You didn't like that?' Sam said. 'You gotta get freed by the funky fresh jazz beast.'

Eric walked up and said something about Billy Collins.

'Billy Collins is dead,' Jordan said. 'He died a week ago.'

'No he didn't,' Eric said. 'Fuck off.'

Aubrey held up the canvas she was painting. The painting was of a deformed looking person. 'It's Eric,' she said.

'The sagging lip represents years of untreated alcoholism,' Jordan said.

Sam sat at the drum set. The carrot-guy walked over and played guitar. His carrot was gone.

Eric walked up to Jordan and said he had a confession. Eric said he never received money from the U.S. government for being one-eighth Native American.

Jordan ignored Eric and looked out the back window. 'There's a fire out there,' he said. 'Let's go.'

*

The fire was big. There was a small tree next to the fire. Kim walked outside and stood next to Jordan and Eric. 'This is how white people die,' she said.

'White people die in Iraq,' Eric said. 'Chill the fuck out.'

Someone threw an onion in the fire. 'Burn the onion,' someone yelled.

'Is that an onion?' Kim said.

'It's okay,' Jordan said. 'We're going to get high.'

'Who started this fire?' Eric said.

'Banksy,' Jordan said.

'Capitalism is the fire, and the tree is the people,' Eric said.

'When Bernie Sanders becomes president I'm going to request that all parties have large fires and Adderall,' Kim said. Jordan gave her an Adderall on the drive over.

Kim talked about moving to Portland. Everyone was always talking about moving to Portland.

Jordan didn't have anything to say about moving to Portland. 'We need to burn this tree,' he said, because it felt like it was his turn to say something.

'It's alive,' Eric said. 'It won't burn.'

'We need to burn the tree,' Jordan said. He was drunk.

'I'm not going to burn the tree,' Eric said.

'Okay,' Jordan said. 'Don't burn the tree.'

'I'm not going to,' Eric said.

'Good,' Jordan said.

Someone threw a pallet on the fire. The fire got bigger. There were about twenty people outside, talking in groups of three or four.

*

A little later Robert showed up to the party. Everyone was still standing around the fire. Robert was wearing his Winn-Dixie apron.

'Why are you still wearing that?' Eric said.

'I forgot,' Robert said.

'Keep it on,' Jordan said. 'It's good.'

Jordan asked Robert when he was going to bring him

some ham-steak.

Robert said the ham-steak at Winn-Dixie wasn't on sale anymore. One time Robert and Jordan got stoned and ate ham-steak on the kitchen floor of Jordan's apartment. Jordan said the ham-steak was shaped like a dog's head and Robert got scared and threw the ham-steak in the freezer, only to be discovered months later.

'They sound kind of good in there,' Robert said about the people playing instruments inside.

'Should we go inside?' Jordan said.

'Take off your apron,' Eric said.

Robert took off his apron. He threw it in the fire.

'Hell yeah,' Eric said.

Eric, Jordan, Robert, and Kim walked inside. They stood in the living room.

There were about twenty people in the living room. They listened to people play music. No one was singing. Jordan walked to the microphone, sang a song about ham-steak and Bernie Sanders. He walked outside, stumbling a little. A person walked past Jordan. 'What is on your shoulder?' Jordan said. 'A hamster?'

The person said it was a rat. Jordan asked if he could pet the rat, and the person said yes. 'Her name is Little Miss,' the person said.

'Hey Little Miss,' Jordan said. He looked at the rat. It had big eyes. 'This rat likes you a lot. You can achieve things.'

'Okay,' the person said. 'Thank you.'

Robert and Eric walked outside. Robert talked about leaving the party to go see a rapper named Kevin Gates. 'I don't want to see Kevin Gates,' Eric said. 'He fucked his cousin.' Robert said that it was cool to fuck your cousin in the year 2015. Jordan went pee behind a dumpster near the garage and then walked inside the garage. The garage was the rat-person's art studio. The rat-person was inside. Jordan said he liked the art. The rat-person said it was shitty beach art he got commissioned to make for rich white people.

Little Miss was in a cage hanging from the ceiling. Jordan put his finger inside the rat cage, and the rat licked his finger. Jordan asked if the rat was going to bite him and the person said no. 'It's licking me,' Jordan said. He walked outside the garage and back inside the house. Someone said something about a terrorist attack in Paris. Olivia was singing and playing tambourine. Sam was asleep on the couch. Robert handed Jordan a beer and they both shotgunned a beer.

*

About a month later Jordan and Robert sat on a twin mattress in Jordan's living room. It was the only furniture in the room. One time Jordan's air-conditioner caught on fire and the firefighters came and asked if his apartment was a squat. He had lived there for six months and still hadn't bought furniture.

Robert played Daniel Johnston on his phone. 'I like how depressed this song makes me feel,' he said.

'Maybe we should do something,' Jordan said. They tried to think of something to do. They said they should either walk to a bar, go to an Asian massage parlor, go see an all-girl Pavement cover band called Babement, drive to Georgia to buy 40-ounces, spend all their money at Red Lobster, or smoke marijuana on the porch. They decided to spend all their money at Red Lobster then Aubrey texted Robert and told them to come over. They picked up some beer at the corner store, then drove on the highway with the windows down and drank beer and listened to Leftover Crack.

*

At Aubrey's house Jordan, Robert, and Olivia sat inside and drank beer and smoked marijuana. They tried to think of something to do. They said they should either drive to a batting cage or start a punk band. They sat outside on lawn chairs in the driveway and smoked marijuana. A Kia Rio with a missing rear-view mirror pulled into the driveway. Eric got out of the car and a beer can fell out.

Eric said he thought about driving into a tree while listening to emo music on the drive over. They sat and talked. They shared drug stories. Robert talked about snorting hydrocodone when he was in high school. Jordan said he accidentally took one of his dachshund's hydrocodones in the eighth grade instead of taking one of his grandma's hydrocodones. Aubrey said she took three gravity bong hits of spice in high school and got naked in the shower and thought about her parents finding her dead. Jordan said he smoked salvia every day for a month in the ninth grade when his friend used his mom's credit card to order salvia off the internet. Robert talked about the time him and Jordan drove into trash cans for fun after a Surfer Blood show, and then decided to only take Ubers for the rest of their lives. Olivia talked about taking an Uber on her way back from an LCD Soundsystem show at 4 a.m. in Miami while high on cocaine. Aubrey talked about peaking on LSD while taking an Uber to an AirBnB in Atlanta. Jordan said they should put his storage closet on AirBnB. Aubrey said she wanted to be an Uber driver so she can quit her job at Starbucks but that her car is too shitty for Ubering. Everyone said she should quit her job at Starbucks. Robert said that Aubrey should get a job at Waffle House.

'Let's all go to Waffle House,' Jordan said.

'Let's go to Waffle House,' Olivia said.

'Let's go to Waffle House everybody,' Robert said.

'Everybody now,' Robert said. He started singing 'This Little Light of Mine' and everyone sang along. They stopped singing. It was quiet for a minute. 'Why does my life suck?' Robert said.

'Let's mix Busch, Tecate, and PBR,' Jordan said.

'We'll take over the craft beer community,' Robert said.

'We'll make merchandise,' Eric said. 'We'll sell flip-flops with bottle-openers in the soles.'

Jordan mixed Busch, Tecate, and PBR. He handed Robert the beer. 'Why do I have to drink it first?' Robert said.

Jordan picked up the beer and drank a little. 'It's really good,' he said.

Eric drank a little. 'It's refreshing,' he said. 'And complex.'

Robert drank a little. 'Wow,' he said. 'I can taste the alcohol.'

No one said anything for a minute.

'Do any stores in Jacksonville sell Faygo?' Eric said.

'The corner store,' Robert said. 'Can we go to Waffle House now?'

'I'm not drunk enough for Waffle House,' Eric said.

'I have to work at six in the morning,' Aubrey said.

Robert said he would buy Aubrey a dozen Waffle House waffles if she quit her job. Olivia said Aubrey should quit her job the same way Kevin Spacey quit his job in *American Beauty*. Aubrey said she thought about that scene sometimes, and it made her want to quit her job. Robert said he had a story. He said he went to the bathroom at Winn-Dixie and there was Fruit of the Loom underwear covered in shit in the middle of the bathroom. He called underwear 'jock wranglers,' and said he made it up. He asked Aubrey if she hated him and thought he was an asshole, and she said no. 'I feel like you think I'm an asshole,' he said.

'Stop,' Jordan said. 'No one thinks you're an asshole.'

'It's okay,' Aubrey said. 'I think I'm an asshole sometimes.'

'Can we all be friends and drink PBR?' Robert said, and they all cheered to nothing and drank PBR.

*

An hour later they ran out of beer. Jordan, Robert, and Olivia got in Jordan's car and drove to Waffle House and ate food. Robert paid for everyone's food. In the car after Waffle House he asked Jordan why he always spent all his money when he got drunk. Jordan said he didn't know. Robert drove Jordan's car. He drove up a steep bridge over the St. Johns River. He looked at Jordan. Jordan thought Robert looked extremely drunk. He was having trouble keeping his head up. 'Are we just going up right now?' Robert said to Jordan.

'We're on a bridge,' Jordan said frantically. 'We're on a bridge, man.' A cop drove next to them.

'Fuck,' Robert said. 'What should I do?'

'Just drive like normal,' Jordan said.

'Should we pull over and sleep?'

'We're almost home.'

At the apartment Jordan and Robert laid on the mattress in the living room. 'I'm glad we're not in that fucking car anymore,' Robert said. He played Daniel Johnston on his phone.

*

A few days later Jordan was at work when he got a text from Emma: We're officially evicted.

Emma said they had until the end of the month to move out. It was December 3rd. Jordan walked out back and sat on the loading dock and stared at the river. He didn't know why they were getting evicted. They hadn't been loud since their last noise complaint. He remembered that his friend, Ethan, had a spare bedroom open for $270 a month. He called Emma, and said they could live together with Ethan for $135 a month each.

'Um, I'm thinking about moving back home with my parents to like, save money.'

'It's only a hundred and thirty-five dollars a month.' Her parents lived in St. Augustine. 'And St. Augustine is so far.'

'I'll have to think about it.'

Jordan said okay.

'Are you upset?'

He said no. He tried to think of something to say.

'I love you,' Emma said.

'I love you, too.' He hung up the phone. He sat in his car and thought about what would happen between him and Emma in the future, not really feeling good or bad about the possibility of them not living together and eventually breaking up, or of them living together and remaining in a relationship.

*

A few hours later Jordan walked to a gym a few blocks from his apartment. He jogged a mile on the treadmill. He did push-ups. He drove home and took a shower. He walked into his bedroom and saw Emma sitting on the bed, reading the eviction letter.

'Have you thought about living at Ethan's?'

Emma said she had, but that she was going to move back in with her parents to save money.

Jordan said okay. Emma said she was going to get a new job in St. Augustine. 'Do you want the cat?' she said.

Jordan said no. He walked into the kitchen and grabbed the lease. He walked into the bedroom. He read, 'The owner may terminate this agreement by giving not less than thirty days written move out notice prior to the last day of the month.' He put the lease on the floor.

*

Later that night Jordan stared into his refrigerator. There wasn't much food in the fridge. He grabbed peanut butter, grape jelly, and flour tortillas. He made a PB&J taco. It was something he started doing one week when he spent all his money on beer. He ate them a lot now. He walked into the bedroom and Emma said they should order pizza. Jordan held up his PB&J taco. 'I'm already eating this,' he said. Emma said that he shouldn't eat so many PB&J tacos. Jordan said PB&J tacos were a good snack. Emma told Jordan to throw the taco away and eat pizza with her. Jordan looked at the PB&J taco. He said okay. Jordan got on a website to order pizza. There was a 'special requests' box on the website.

'Special requests?' he said to Emma.

'Wear a funny hat.'

'That's funny. Is that from TV?'

'No.'

'You thought of that?'

'Yeah,' Emma said. 'I'm funny sometimes.'

Jordan typed 'wear funny hat' into the 'special requests' box.

Jordan's computer said it was running on 'reserve battery power.'

'I'm running on reserve battery power,' Jordan said. 'We all have problems.'

'I'm running on reserve battery power,' Emma said and laughed.

'I just said that.'

'I said that.'

'I just said it, too,' Jordan said. 'Before you.'

'I said we're running on reserve battery power.'

'That's what I said.'

'You said we all have problems.'

'Yeah. I said that, too.'

'You didn't say it.'

'I did.'

'Don't take credit for my joke,' Emma said and made a face.

'I swear I said that.'

They didn't talk for a minute.

'My face smells like your ass,' Jordan said without thinking.

'Kanye West had a baby today,' Jordan said. 'I tried to get the twitter handle @saintwest, but someone already got it. I was gonna sell the handle and drop out of college and never worry about money again.'

'That's dumb,' Emma said. 'Wanna watch *The Office*?'

'I don't like *The Office*,' Jordan said. 'I don't derive pleasure from watching TV shows,' he said in monotone.

'That's insane,' Emma said. 'Everyone likes *The Office*. Wanna watch *Billy on the Street*?'

'Not really.'

'What *do* you want?' Emma said in a voice.

'I don't know,' Jordan said. 'But I don't wanna watch a celebrity harass strangers.'

'You liked it last time.'

'I was stoned.'

'I forgot you were stoned,' Emma said. 'I'm sleepy.' She stood and walked into the bathroom. Jordan walked into the living room. He looked at Emma peeing. 'Bring me the cat,' Emma said while peeing.

'You're peeing.'

'No,' Emma said. 'When I get up.'

'Oh,' Jordan said. 'So you can get him yourself then.'

Emma made a loud disapproving noise. Jordan laughed. 'Just kidding,' he said, and brought Emma the cat. 'Here's your cat.'

The cat ran away as soon as Jordan sat it down. 'Come back,' Emma yelled at the cat. Jordan and Emma went and lay in bed.

'What's the Netflix password?' Emma said.

Jordan told Emma the Netflix password. The cat walked into the bedroom. The cat's name was Wilbur. It was a stupid fucking cat. Jordan stared at it. 'You look stupid,' he said. 'You're the dumbest human being on the Earth. Get a job. At Subway. And wear shoes.'

The cat jumped back on the bed. Emma sat up in bed. She touched the cat, and he jumped off the bed again.

'Fuck you,' Emma said.

'He launched,' Jordan said. 'Where am I going to

live? You're leaving me.'

'Have you started looking for an apartment yet?'

'I'm going to a party Ethan is going to next week and he's going to show me the bedroom after. But I might just live at the bottom of the St. Johns River in my Honda Element. Do you want a Cobb salad for Christmas?'

Emma said yes.

Jordan heard a knock at the door.

'If he's not wearing a funny hat then pay for the pizza with a cat,' Jordan said like he was reciting a nursery rhyme.

Emma stood and walked downstairs. She walked back upstairs holding pizza.

'He wasn't wearing a hat,' she said.

'Fuck him,' Jordan said, and they ate pizza on the bed.

*

A couple days later Jordan sat at the picnic table near the library with Eric and Aubrey.

'One thousand nine elevens,' Eric said while staring at his feet, smoking a cigarette.

'I wanna smoke crack before class,' Jordan said.

'I don't wanna smoke crack,' Eric said. 'Every drug I've ever done has turned into a problem for me.'

'If you wanna be a bohemian you have to smoke crack,' Jordan said.

'Don't smoke crack,' Aubrey said.

'I'm not going to smoke crack,' Eric said. 'Fuck off.'

'I know you won't,' Aubrey said. 'But don't. You're a functioning addict. Low-functioning addict.'

'Mid-functioning,' Eric said. 'Depending on what

33

your definition of functioning is. Girls still talk to me. Why do they do that?'

'What do I have to do to get an Adderall?' Aubrey said.

'Why do you need an Adderall?'

'I have to write an essay about plumpy nuts in Africa, for my foreign culture class.'

'I'm taking politics of France next semester,' Jordan said.

'Eagles of defeating ISIS,' Eric said. He shit-talked an article he read on Vice. Eric was always shit-talking Vice.

'I'm tired of shit-talking Vice,' Jordan said.

'Jordan is moody,' Eric said.

Aubrey typed something into her phone. She showed Jordan a picture of a capybara sitting next to a small dog in a kiddie pool.

'That's nice,' Jordan said. 'I'm not moody anymore. Thank you.' He looked at Eric. 'Do you think Robert would want to go eat food with me, at the café?'

'I don't know,' Eric said. 'But I know a dishwasher with twelve fingers that works in the dish pit there. He smokes a lot of weed. He puts his second pinky nub into the pinky hole of pipes. He wiggled it for me once. I didn't ask for that.'

'I'd chop off my pinky nubs,' Jordan said.

'He's a bad dishwasher,' Eric said. 'He's so high.'

'I'm always high at work,' Aubrey said.

'I would get stoned and stare at my hands if I had twelve fingers,' Jordan said.

'Hey girl, you wanna feel my nubby finger?' Eric said in a sexual voice. 'It looks just like a clitoris but more flexible. I wanna go to a porn store and buy whip-its.'

'I can get a cracker from Starbucks,' Aubrey said. 'Also whip-its.'

'Do that on your last day,' Eric said.

'I don't think I wanna do whip-its,' Jordan said. 'No, I'll do them. I'll just feel stupid.'

'Is that why I was a shitty person in high school?' Eric said. 'Because I did whip-its?'

'Doesn't ecstasy make a hole in your brain?'

'All drugs make holes in your brain,' Eric said. 'The guy we bought whip-its from in high school made everyone call him Squid.'

'Squid,' Aubrey said.

'He got a job at GameStop and his nametag said *Jake McSnake*. It's a really convoluted saga, like a John Irving type of tale.'

No one said anything for a minute. Aubrey and Eric lit another cigarette.

'When's the last time you guys played laser tag?' Eric said. 'I'm being serious.'

'I played air hockey the other day,' Aubrey said.

'I played glow-in-the-dark putt-putt with Robert a while ago,' Jordan said. 'Then we ate churros at Taco Bell. It was a good day.'

'I know,' Eric said. 'I wanted to go, but I had to work.'

'Can we go to a batting cage?' Aubrey said.

'I don't want to pay dollars to be bad at something,' Eric said. 'I don't have many dollars. Fun Station used to have bumper boats. That was fun.'

'Bumper boats are scary,' Aubrey said.

'I used to think that I would fall overboard and get torn up by the propeller,' Jordan said.

'That's the way of the high sea, sailor,' Eric said. He flicked his cigarette. 'You must be at least this scurvy to ride.'

'I wish the library wasn't packed,' Jordan said.

'We can just go to my house and study,' Aubrey said.

'That sounds horrible,' Eric said. 'You sound horrible.' He lit another cigarette. 'I hope ISIS kills Bono.' Eric's phone rang. 'Hello, is this Al Qaeda? Yeah. We're at the smoking table.' He hung up his phone. 'Robert is coming.'

'How long can we text about joining ISIS until I start to feel watched by the U.S. government?' Jordan said. 'I don't want to have to explain to my parents why the government thought I was in ISIS.'

'I'm going to bomb Florida back into the ocean,' Eric said.

'I don't know why ISIS hasn't bombed Disney World,' Aubrey said. 'So many innocent civilians.'

'Are they really innocent if they're at Disney World though?' Jordan said. 'Banksy doesn't think so.'

'Fuck you,' Eric said. 'You won't talk about Vice, but you'll talk about Banksy. I hate you.'

'I'm pretty sure Vice has a documentary about him,' Aubrey said.

Robert walked up to the table. He was wearing a jean jacket with an Operation Ivy patch, and a Carnival Cruise hat with a Choking Victim patch sewn over the Carnival logo. He had a mohawk rat-tail combination.

'You look like a punk-rocking monster truck driver,' Eric said.

'I am,' Robert said. 'Corporate rock sucks. Can I bum a cigarette?'

Eric gave Robert a cigarette. Aubrey talked about a Vice documentary where a person takes acid and goes to a monster truck rally.

'I'm taking a semester off to drive around the country in a monster truck,' Robert said. 'Not really. But I am taking a semester off to drive around the country in a Honda Accord my parents bought me.'

'Really?' Jordan said.

'Yeah,' Robert said. 'I've got some family up in Baltimore.'

'What are we gonna do without you?' Eric said.

'I don't know,' Robert said. 'You'll have to suck your own wieners.'

*

Around 1 a.m. that night Eric texted Jordan, 'I'm stressed.' Jordan was lying in bed, reading stupid bullshit on his phone. Emma was asleep next to him.

'Why?' Jordan texted.

'Much less about finals and much more how futile college feels most of the time.'

'Yeah?'

'I could have been living on a mountain these last three years, learning how to hunt bears for sustenance. I could live a quaint life cooking ribs in a timeshare community. I met a guy in North Carolina that smoked beans and sausages in a restaurant on stilts over a river. And I think: Why not that life? I'm still young. I could do that.'

'After college we can be bohemians,' Jordan texted.

'I'll be Ginsberg, you be Kerouac.'

'I watched the greatest minds of my generation do whip-its in a Big Lots parking lot. In all seriousness though, the alternatives to not being bohemians seem stupid.'

'You are right completely.'

'401K,' Jordan texted. 'Young Bukowski trap lord.'

'Dividends,' Eric texted.

'Samisms,' Jordan texted. Sam was about to graduate

and make $55,000 a year doing engineering stuff on roads. He talked about his credit score sometimes.

'I knew it,' Eric texted. 'Tell him to go home and sleep it off.'

'What are you talking about?'

'I thought you were hanging out with Sam.'

'No. You're being absurd. Does your ass ever itch for no reason?'

'Kim keeps kicking me but the only itch I have is on my foot, like under my toenail. Am I dying? Is this how it all concludes, over a ranch salad and Miller High Life?'

'I knew High Life would be in the equation. Ranch is a wild card.'

'I had that realization recently,' Eric texted. 'It's the champagne of beers.'

'That's an ironic marketing ploy by an evil corporation.'

'Shut up,' Eric texted. 'Should we smoke crack-cocaine?'

'I do want crack.'

'Jordan.'

'Will you get addicted though?'

'Are we going to smoke crack?' Eric texted.

'I will smoke crack.'

'I want to get shrooms or acid. Kim can find some.'

'Do that,' Jordan texted. 'Let's get cross faded on crack-cocaine and LSD. We will reach enlightenment. David Lynch will give us trophies and take us to Cheesecake Factory for Blue Moons and fried mac and cheese. I want to smoke crack.'

'I'll think on it seriously,' Eric texted. 'Let's smoke acid and do mescaline.'

'Okay we will do crack then.'

'I don't want to do crack but if it were offered I would not say no,' Eric texted.

'Okay then that's the plan: only smoke crack when offered.'

'Yes perfect.'

'Reading about crack on Wikipedia,' Jordan texted. 'Seems promising.'

'Let's binge for three days.'

'I will do that,' Eric texted. 'College is for this.'

'Excited,' Jordan texted. 'I'm going to bed. Goodnight.'

'Goodnight.'

*

A few days later Jordan got off work around 9 p.m. He drove to the corner store and bought a twelve pack of beer. He drove to an address that Ethan sent him. It was a few blocks from his current apartment. Jordan parked his car on the side of the road, and saw Ethan sitting on the porch with Daniel and Abby. Daniel was Ethan's roommate and Abby was Daniel's ex-girlfriend. Jordan met them at a Halloween party Ethan hosted. They were dating at the time. Jordan talked to Ethan, Abby, and Daniel for a few minutes then walked inside to put his beer in the fridge. There were about a dozen people inside. Jordan didn't know most of them. He walked through the living room into the kitchen. The Republican primary debates were playing on a projector and everyone at the party was taking shots of whiskey or drinking beer when the candidates said or did certain things. Jordan put his beer in the fridge then walked back outside and sat around a small table. He drank beer and listened to Abby and Daniel argue about gun control. Daniel was pro-guns. He owned guns and liked to shoot them. Abby said she was tired of arguing about gun control and said she was going to order a pizza. When the pizza arrived Jordan walked inside to grab beer for everyone. Sara asked him to sit next to her on the couch. Jordan thought she seemed drunk. He knew Sara from the Halloween party, too. She was dressed up as the heroin lady from *Pulp Fiction*. Sara asked him when the pizza was coming, and he said the pizza was outside. A vegan lady that Jordan had never met before said something about pepperonis and animal grease. Jordan said the pizza was cheese. The vegan lady said cheese wasn't vegan. He stared at the projection and listened to Rand Paul yell about net neutrality. Rand Paul said something stupid and Sara told Jordan he had to take a shot of whiskey. Jordan didn't like taking shots, but liked whiskey, and didn't want to seem uptight, so he took the shot. He walked back outside. Ethan was yelling about politics with a mouthful of pizza.

'I'm voting for Jeb Bush,' Jordan said. 'His dumb-ass dad was president and his dumb-ass brother was president and now it's his dumb-ass turn to be president.'

Daniel laughed. He said he was going to write in Waka Flocka, a rapper from Atlanta that released a video on 4/20, jokingly announcing that he was running for president, and was going to legalize marijuana, keep dogs out of restaurants, and raise the federal minimum wage.

Sara walked outside and grabbed a slice of pizza. 'I'm gonna go inside and watch Donald Trump say stupid bullshit and eat pizza,' she said.

Sara walked inside, and her boyfriend, Tom, walked outside. 'Three people want pizza,' he said. He picked up the box without asking and walked back inside the house. Daniel made a face and yelled 'Tom,' three times. Each time he yelled *Tom* he yelled it louder. Tom shut the door without acknowledging Daniel, and Daniel yelled, 'Let me get a slice,' as he stood and walked toward the door. Daniel followed Tom inside in the house. Jordan heard a loud noise then heard two or three people simultaneously yell, 'Stop.' A few seconds later, Daniel walked outside the house. He looked confused and frightened. 'Don't come back in,' Tom yelled, and slammed the door.

'You didn't pay, faggot,' Daniel said.

Jordan heard Tom say, 'He punched me.'

'Why did you punch Tom?' Ethan said.

'I pushed him down.'

Tom opened the door again and yelled, 'Don't come back ever again. Just leave. Leave now. I'm not kidding. Get off my porch,' then in a demon-like voice he yelled, 'Get the fuck off my porch.'

'Alright,' Daniel said. 'Stop yelling.'

Tom slammed the door.

No one said anything for a minute. Abby said she was going to see if Tom was okay and walked inside.

'I didn't think it was that serious,' Ethan said.

'I need to grab my cooler,' Daniel said.

'He was very angry,' Ethan said.

'It's the debates,' Jordan said. He felt uncomfortable.

Ethan stood and said he was going to grab a slice of pizza and Daniel's cooler. He turned the door knob. 'It's locked,' he said.

The vegan lady came to the door and made a face through the glass.

'I have no idea what happened,' Ethan said.

'That was really fucked up,' the vegan lady said.

'He's leaving,' Ethan said.

'But you're his roommate.'

'Yes,' Ethan said. 'That's a true statement.'

'What?' Jordan said.

'We're roommates,' Ethan said.

'Shit,' Jordan said. 'My beer is in there.'

The vegan lady opened the door and Abby walked outside.

'Why did Daniel punch Tom in the face?' she said.

'I don't know,' Ethan said, then walked inside the house.

Jordan stood and walked inside. He petted a medium-sized dog and felt calm and removed from the situation. He accidentally knocked over a small dancing Christmas tree onto the floor. The batteries fell out of the Christmas tree, and people looked at him and he felt self-conscious and out of place. He wasn't drunk enough. He picked up the dancing Christmas tree, put the batteries inside the plastic base, and then walked outside the house without grabbing his beer. Ethan, Abby, and Jordan walked toward Daniel's car. Daniel was seated in the driver's seat.

'Don't call people faggots,' Abby said while crossing the road, barely avoiding getting hit by a car.

'You're gonna die,' Ethan said.

'I'm fine. I'm not dying tonight. People drive so fucking fast down this street. Don't call people faggots.'

'Stop being all high and mighty,' Daniel said.

'I'm not being high and mighty. Don't call people faggots. It's not cool. Especially when they have a girlfriend. Don't call people faggots.'

'That was probably the thing that set him off,' Ethan said.

'I shouldn't have called him a faggot,' Daniel said.

Jordan saw a car driving slowly down the road. He

held up his beer to the car. 'Good speed,' he said.

'I like this little guy,' Abby said, and hugged Jordan. He didn't have time to reciprocate the hug. Daniel squinted at Jordan.

'His name is Jordan,' Ethan said.

'I know his name,' Abby said.

'You called him a little guy.'

'That's okay,' Jordan said.

Another car sped by and almost hit Abby. 'I'm going to fucking die,' she said.

Daniel said he was going back to the house. He drove away.

Jordan, Ethan, and Abby walked back to Tom's because Abby forgot her purse. The door was locked again. 'Can I get my purse?' Abby said through the glass.

Sara came to the door and opened it. 'Tom is very upset,' she said.

'We know,' Ethan said.

'Tom is upset because Daniel punched him in the face.'

'We get it,' Abby said. 'Trust me. We get it. He's my ex-boyfriend.'

'Daniel is dumb and I hate him,' Sara said.

Abby asked why Daniel punched Tom in the face.

'Because pizza,' Jordan said.

Sara let them inside the house and Jordan walked toward the fridge to grab his beer. The beer wasn't in the fridge.

'I'm not trying to be rude,' the vegan lady said. 'But Tom really wants you three to leave. Do you guys have everything you need, so you can leave?'

'I'm sure Tom is fine with them,' Sara said. 'He's just not fine with Daniel.'

'He just said he wants them gone,' the vegan lady said.

'Is all the beer gone?' Jordan said.

'I don't know,' the vegan lady said.

'Okay,' Jordan said. 'Nice to meet you guys.'

'That was bizarre,' Jordan said outside. 'Someone hid my beer.'

'Fuck,' Abby said. 'I forgot the whiskey.'

'I'll get it,' Ethan said.

Tom walked from behind the house, onto the front law, and stared at Jordan, Ethan, and Abby. He looked annoyed. 'Guys I really want you to leave,' he said. 'I'm sorry.'

'We're leaving,' Ethan said. 'We keep forgetting shit inside. The whiskey is in the house.'

'Get the Fireball and bring it out to them,' Tom said to the vegan lady, in a tone like he was a king, calmly instructing one of his subjects to arbitrarily execute a peasant.

'Thank you,' Ethan said. Tom walked away without responding.

'What the fuck,' Ethan said, and flipped off Tom to his back.

'I'm gonna go to Birdies,' Abby said. Birdies was a shitty dive bar in Five Points. 'Keep my Fireball.'

Ethan made a face at Abby. 'It's okay,' Jordan said. 'Let's go.'

Sara walked outside with the Fireball. 'I don't want it,' Abby said. 'Give it to Ethan. I don't want it.'

Sara handed the Fireball to Ethan. 'I feel super awkward,' Sara said.

'You should feel super awkward,' Ethan said. 'This is a super awkward situation. This is extremely awkward.' Jordan thought Ethan was being dramatic. He walked toward the edge of the sidewalk and made a quiet, low-pitched noise.

*

Ethan and Jordan got inside Jordan's car and drove down College Street toward Ethan's house, a mile away, across the railroad tracks, in a poorer part of downtown called Murray Hill.

'That was confusing,' Jordan said. 'I don't know any of those people.'

'I had sex with Sara while her and Tom were dating but he only knows about us making out,' Ethan said. 'So he doesn't like me I guess.'

'Oh,' Jordan said. 'That makes sense.'

They crossed the railroad track and drove past a strip mall with a Metro PCS, Subway, Family Dollar, laundromat, and a charter school. 'I can't wait to eat Subway and educate myself,' Jordan said, not wanting to listen to Ethan talk about having sex with Sara anymore.

'That Family Dollar is my shit. The beer selection is awful though.'

'Was Abby really drunk or does she always drawl out her words like that?'

'She always talks like that,' Ethan said. 'Abby is cool.'

*

'We got kicked out, too,' Ethan said to Daniel. Daniel was sitting on the couch drinking a beer, looking at his phone.

'I feel like I handled that situation well,' Daniel said without looking up from his phone.

Jordan thought, 'Except for punching Tom in the face.'

Daniel stopped looking at his phone. He stood. 'Let me show you the room,' he said.

*

'Welcome to the humblest of abodes,' Daniel said in a weird voice, gesturing toward the room. It was a little bigger than a closet.

'Nice,' Jordan said. 'It's really small. I like it.'

Daniel turned on a fan in the corner of the room. 'This is the dankest,' he said and turned on the fan. 'It gets hot in here so I'll let you keep it.' The room was on the other side of the fireplace.

'Powerful,' Jordan said.

'Yeah, uh, that's about it,' Daniel said. 'Do you want a beer?'

'Sure.' Jordan, Daniel, and Ethan sat on the couch and drank beer.

'So who really won the republican debate?' Daniel said and laughed near-hysterically.

'I think we did,' Ethan said.

'I just felt like a spectator,' Jordan said.

*

Around 1:00 a.m. on New Year's Eve, after working a ten hour barback shift, and watching fireworks explode over the river with Emma, Jordan sat alone on Sara's porch while waiting for his friend, Slime—who was visiting from Gainesville, where he attended UF as a political science senior—to arrive with an unspecified number of people, who were all returning from the bars in Five Points to continue partying at the house. Jordan noticed Slime walking drunkenly, about twenty-feet ahead of everyone else. He was wearing an oversized cardigan with no shirt underneath and holding a Donald Trump 2016 sign in each hand. 'I missed you so much,' Slime said and threw the Trump signs on the ground, then hugged Jordan tightly, for about thirty seconds, sporadically kissing him on the cheek.

*

'How are you and Emma?' Slime said a few minutes later. They were standing in the kitchen. Slime stirred some leftover pho he stole from the fridge. Kayla, Slime's girlfriend, was standing next to him.

'Good, I think,' Jordan said. He hadn't hung out with Emma except at work in over a week. She was living back at home with her parents. Jordan had moved into Ethan's place a few days ago.

'Remember when we listened to David Bowie?' Slime said. 'And threw the beer bottles at the construction site behind your dorm? God dammit, Jordan. I miss you so much. Seriously—' Slime used to go to UNF. He felt depressed and thought transferring to a better school would help.

'Are you graduating soon?' Kayla said.

Jordan laughed. He felt sober. He stole a couple beers from the cooler at work around midnight but other than that he hadn't drank any alcohol yet. 'I miss you too, Slime. And yeah, I have like, one more semester.'

'What are you gonna do?' Kayla said.

He thought about making a suicide joke. 'I'll probably just keep working in restaurants.'

Slime put the bowl up to his face and loudly slurped

noodles.

'You ate the last noodle,' Kayla said. 'What kind of boyfriend are you?'

'The shitty kind,' Slime said with a mouthful of noodles. 'Fuck. We're out of noodles.'

'You ate so much,' Kayla said.

Slime picked up a bowl of popcorn off the stove and grabbed a handful. He shoved the popcorn in his mouth and chewed aggressively, with his mouth open.

'Jesus,' Kayla said. 'Where are you living now, Jordan?'

'I just moved in with Ethan, like...a week ago.'

Slime made a noise like he was gagging on his popcorn. 'Ethan is a sociopath,' he said and walked out the back door.

'Just don't lend him money,' Kayla said. Jordan had already given him money. Three hundred dollars for an abortion. 'He's funny but kind of an asshole.' Kayla walked out the back door and Jordan followed. Slime wasn't on the back porch.

'Does anyone know where the cute hairy man in the cardigan went?' Kayla said.

Someone pointed at the stairs and Jordan and Kayla walked down the stairs.

Slime was sitting on the bottom step, resting his forehead against the handrail. His cardigan was unbuttoned. He looked like he was about to puke.

'You're alive,' Jordan said. 'Happy News Years.'

'Jordan,' Slime said. 'God dammit. You're living with Ethan, man. I feel betrayed. You're supposed to sleep with me in Gainesville.'

'I don't go to UF though.'

'I know, but you'd have a place. You'd have a place any fucking day. Hey Kayla, Jordan could stay with us.

He could sleep on the futon.'

'I thought we were gonna move to New York,' Jordan said.

'Yes,' Slime yelled.

'Same,' Kayla said.

'I clean my dishes,' Slime said. 'I wash my plates. I love David Bowie. You know we get along. You know I clean my dishes. You know I clean my plates. You know I love David Bowie.'

'Let's get bunk beds,' Jordan said.

'Let's move to New York with all of our friends and get bunk beds,' Kayla said.

'Shut up,' Slime said. 'I'm living with Jordan.'

'Don't say that,' Jordan said. 'We can all live together.'

'Touch penises,' Slime said. 'I'm drunk. I'm sorry. We ain't gonna touch peens.'

'We can touch penises if you want.'

'Count yourself out,' Slime said to Kayla.

'Should we buy more beer?' Jordan said.

'I'm drunk as fuck,' Slime said. 'I'm really drunk. I'm fucked up.'

'I'm going inside,' Kayla said.

'No, Kayla. Please. Kayla, please.'

'Slime,' Jordan said.

'I'm pretty drunk,' Slime said.

'I'm going to sleep,' Kayla said.

'I'm drunk as fuck.'

'We can sleep at Ethan's.'

'He's going to harass.'

'We should sleep at Ethan's,' Kayla said. 'We should sleep at Jordan's house.'

'It's Ethan's house,' Slime said.

'I'm going to sleep on the couch then,' Kayla said.

'Tom said we could sleep at his house.'

'That's fine,' Slime said. 'As long as it's not Ethan's. He's going to harass.'

'I love Ethan,' Kayla said.

'He raped me,' Slime said. 'I'm just kidding. He didn't rape me. He wanted to fuck you.'

'Before I met you,' Kayla said.

Slime made a low-pitched, cow-sounding noise. 'Let's sleep at Tom's house,' he said. 'It's like, two blocks away.'

'I'm gonna go home and eat a pomegranate,' Jordan said.

Slime kicked the handrail.

'You just broke that,' Kayla said.

Slime laughed near-hysterically. 'They shouldn't have invited me. They knew it was going to happen. Where's the alcohol? Go home and eat a pomegranate. Jesus, Jordan, it's 2016.'

'I think we're out of beer,' Kayla said.

Slime stood quickly and walked drunkenly up the stairs and into the house.

'Normally I'm just as drunk as he is so this isn't a problem but he's so drunk that I feel less drunk,' Kayla said. 'Maybe I should get drunker.' She said this in voice that someone might use to casually discuss potential, long-term life plans, like moving to a new city, or applying for grad school.

'Someone drank all the Fat Tires,' Slime yelled, and threw an empty Fat Tire box over the handrail, and almost fell down the stairs.

'I think we drank them,' Kayla said. 'We drank them.'

'No,' Slime said, and yanked a giant leaf off a palmetto tree that was growing over the handrail, then kicked the handrail, and said, sounding accomplished, 'This whole thing is fucked up.'

Jordan asked Slime to sit with him on the front porch. Slime picked up a nearly empty bottle of gin, and said that he would sit on the porch if Jordan let him use his beer as a chaser for gin.

'You're going to throw up,' Jordan said.

'Not me,' Slime said. 'I never do that. I've never done that. I never will. You better give me that beer as a chaser.'

'You just took a shot,' Kayla said.

'No I didn't,' Slime said. He drank some gin. He handed Jordan the gin and Jordan took a drink.

'Can I have the gin?' Kayla said.

'Can I have one more shot first?' Jordan said, feeling like getting drunk suddenly. He remembered reading somewhere that something happens to the brain after ingesting alcohol that makes you want to keep drinking.

Jordan took another drink.

Slime put his head on the grass and made a noise like he was about to throw up, but didn't.

Jordan remembered a video he saw on Facebook, about how binge drinking is glorified in the U.S. — on TV and in movies — but not glorified as much in other countries, where the drinking age is usually lower, and young people are taught to drink in moderation. He felt annoyed that he was thinking about alcohol abuse while drinking alcohol.

Jordan told Slime that he went over the edge and called him Hunter S. Thompson.

Slime botched a Hunter S. Thompson quote, then kicked the vinyl paneling that encircled the house.

'You drank too much,' Kayla said. 'Why are you so destructive?'

'I hate everything,' Slime said.

'You don't hate everything,' Jordan said, and gave Slime a hug.

'I hate a lot of things,' Slime said.

'What do you hate?' Jordan said.

'Wealthy white people,' Slime said.

'What are you going to do?'

'Get wealthy and white,' Slime said and kicked the vinyl paneling.

'I bought him Doc Martens,' Kayla said, and pointed at Slime's boots. 'This is what I get.'

'You're a punk rocker now,' Jordan said. He felt buzzed. He felt less concerned and more amused by Slime's excessive drinking. 'Do you remember when we saw Black Flag?'

'I remember that. Do you remember when you played Mac Demarco for me?' Slime said, then incoherently shit-talked Mac Demarco's fan-base. 'God dammit, Jordan. I miss you.'

Jordan drank more gin. 'I miss you too. Let's sit on the porch.'

Slime made a noise that Jordan thought probably meant, 'Okay.' Jordan and Kayla helped him stand, then helped him walk to the front porch, where he collapsed immediately, rolled onto his back, and opened his cardigan so that his hairy chest and beer belly were exposed. Jordan sat next to Slime, feeling glad that he wasn't inebriated.

'I need to chug water,' Slime said. 'I'm drunk as fuck. I'm gonna be hungover.'

Kayla sat in a rocking chair, and told Jordan to sit in the chair next to her.

Slime stood abruptly and sat in the chair.

'That was rude,' Kayla said.

'Lay on the floor,' Jordan said.

'I don't wanna.'

'You didn't want the chair until I offered it to Jordan. That's what babies do,' Kayla said, more like she was stating a fact than disapproving of Slime's behavior.

'Take off your cardigan,' Jordan said. He wanted to fuck with Slime because he was drunk.

'I'll do anything for daddy,' Slime said. He took off his cardigan slowly. He stuck his tongue out and wiggled it around.

Kayla made a face. 'That was weird,' she said.

'I don't give a fuck,' Slime said. He grabbed his belly and jiggled it. 'That's right. I'm fat.'

'You're not fat,' Jordan said. Slime had definitely gained weight.

'What's your problem?' Slime said.

'I'm just looking at your hot belly.'

'You did well for daddy,' Kayla said.

'What the fuck,' Slime said, and banged his hand on the porch.

'What's wrong?' Kayla said.

'I'm fucked. The world is fucked.'

'Happy New Year,' Jordan said.

'I'm disgusting and I hate myself.'

'Can you make sure Slime doesn't die while I get him water?' Kayla said.

'Yeah,' Jordan said. He took a picture of Slime and sent it to Emma.

*

A couple weeks later Jordan and Eric sat at the picnic table near the library before their fiction workshop class. 'I'm out of cigarettes and don't have any money,' Eric said.

'Grow your own tobacco.'

'I'm going to save my last cigarette for the break. I only work one shift this week. I'm going to steal heads of lettuce from work and only eat heads of lettuce smothered in ranch all week.' Eric lit his cigarette.

'You didn't save it.'

'I'm stupid. I'll bum a cigarette from the professor. I'm going to write a short story about growing my beard out until it touches my toes. My beard is touching my little nipples. It's been thirty years. I get crumbs stuck in my little beard.'

'I put gold in my beard and walk around downtown and make all the boys jealous,' Jordan said in an old man voice.

'I walk around downtown collecting little golden flecks for my beard,' Eric said in the same voice.

'We're insane,' Jordan said.

'I'm a bohemian,' Eric said. 'Living in willful poverty for my erotic fan-fiction.'

Jordan noticed Eric staring at the ground. 'What are you looking at?' he said.

'I'm staring wistfully into an existential abyss. I'm the Zach Braff of the Zach Braff generation. I get jumpy when I'm broke because if something happens to my Kia Rio I won't have money to pay for it and I'll have to drive my Kia Rio into the fucking sun.'

'That's what the Federal Reserve is for,' Jordan said without thinking.

'We should rob the Federal Reserve. I wonder if Aubrey has any cigarettes.'

'I wonder if Robert will be my boyfriend when Emma breaks up with me.'

'My nipples are hard,' Eric said.

'Did you take too much Adderall again?'

'Probably. How are your new roommates doing?'

'They're alright. I let Ethan borrow money from me before someone told me not to let Ethan borrow money from me. Do you ever wish you were autistic?'

'No.'

'They seem happy, and like, they don't worry about anything.'

'Sam's autistic brother eats McNuggets with no breading.'

Jordan stared at people in suits. 'Who do these people think they are?' he said in a voice.

'Posers,' Eric said in the same voice. 'Wall Street fat cats. Bernie will soon imprison everyone that owns a tie.'

'We're idiots.'

'Not me,' Eric said. 'I'm a genius bohemian.' He picked up his empty pack of cigarettes and put the pack in his mouth, pretended to smoke it. 'A delicious, smooth, toasty flavor. Kind of like tin foil.' He threw the pack on the ground.

Jordan stared at the ground. 'There's a packet of mayonnaise under the table.'

Eric and Jordan stared at the mayonnaise. 'I feel like that sometimes,' Eric said.

'That's nice,' Jordan said.

*

A few days later Jordan worked a lunch shift then clocked out. He stood behind the host stand with Emma and rubbed her back while she arranged scissors and pencils in a small cup. He told Emma he was about to leave. They had plans to see a movie the next day. He asked what movie she wanted to see, and Emma said she hadn't checked to see what was playing. A few days ago Jordan told her both movies that were playing, and she said they seemed good. Jordan asked if she wanted to stay the night and Emma said that she had to talk to her mom first. He thought that was weird. He said okay. He went to kiss her and she turned her face to the side and he kissed her cheek. Jordan thought, 'she didn't kiss me.' He thought, 'she didn't kiss me because she's sick,' after remembering that Emma said she might be getting sick. He walked outside and got in his car and drove toward his house. He got a text from Emma while merging onto the highway.

He lay in bed and opened the text: Can I come over after work?

Jordan called Emma. 'Let's just talk right now.'

'I'm at work babe,' Emma said. 'I'll come over after work.'

'You can't do that—'

'I don't wanna do it over the phone.'

'Do what over the phone?'

'I'll come over after work.'

'Just do it right now.'

Emma said okay, and broke up with Jordan.

Jordan said he understood, and that he would talk to her later, and hung up the phone. He stared at the ceiling for a few minutes. He paced around the living room. He walked into the bathroom and turned on the water. He took a long shower. He went on Craigslist and looked at jobs. He threw his car keys at the wall. He ate half an apple. He cried in bed. He called his job. 'Hello, this is Emma thank you for calling Lee Logan's Brewing Company—'

'Can I talk to a manager?'

Emma said yeah.

Jordan was on hold. Shitty jazz was playing.

'Hello?' the manager said.

'It's Jordan. I'm not coming into work tomorrow.'

'Okay,' the manager said and paused. 'Can you come help set up the buffet tomorrow, for like an hour?'

He thought, 'Fuck.' He said sure. He hung up the phone.

He texted Eric and said that he and Emma broke up. He texted Robert the same thing. He sat in his bed. He stared at the floor. He thought that he would focus on eating healthy, exercising regularly, reading books, and trying not to do anything stupid.

*

The next night Jordan sat on Eric's porch with Eric, Olivia, and Sam.

'I wanna get shot in the back of the head with no warning,' Eric said. He drank some beer from the Dough Mahoney glass.

'I'll shoot you,' Olivia said.

'No, don't. I wanna die from a brain aneurysm.' He stared at Sam. 'Hey man, are you a fucking Nazi?'

Sam didn't say anything.

'One of my professors said *Nazis equal socialism*,' Olivia said.

'I didn't know Ted Cruz worked at UNF,' Eric said.

No one said anything for a minute. Olivia smoked marijuana. She offered Jordan some. He said he was okay.

'Have you ever done Quaaludes?' Eric said to Sam.

'It's the jacket,' Olivia said. 'You look like you love Quaaludes.'

'You look like Robin Williams from *Good Will*

57

Hunting,' Eric said.

Sam stared at Eric. 'I'm flipping you off. My hands are in my jacket so you can't see. But I'm flipping you off.'

'I feel it,' Olivia said.

'Am I still flipping you off?' Sam said.

'Yeah,' Olivia said.

'No, I'm not.'

'You are,' Jordan said.

Sam took his hands out of his jacket. He was flipping Jordan off.

'My favorite Jimmy Eat World album is *Clarity* because the entire album is a love letter to social hesitation,' Eric said in a voice.

'Do not make fun of me,' Sam said. 'It's a great album.'

'It's pretty much their *Pinkerton*,' Eric said.

'Thank you,' Sam said. He said something else about Jimmy Eat World.

Eric said that he felt the same way about whatever Sam said about the band Jimmy Eat World. Jordan, Sam, Eric, and Olivia walked inside the apartment. They sat on couches in the living room.

'When's Robert coming home?' Olivia said.

'As soon as he finds God,' Eric said.

'End of February, I think,' Jordan said.

'That's so long.'

'I know,' Jordan said. 'I miss him.'

'I'm getting tired of sucking my own dick,' Eric said.

Eric turned on the TV and pulled up Netflix. He played the show *Scrubs*, starring Zach Braff. 'Did you guys know Dr. Cox was in a movie about Vietnam?' he said.

No one said anything. Eric stood and walked into the

kitchen. He put a t-shirt in the dryer.

Jordan stared at the TV. He saw Zach Braff standing at a urinal next to the janitor. Zach Braff looked over the urinal divider at the janitor's penis. Zach Braff asked the janitor why his pants weren't unzipped. The janitor said he wasn't pissing and that the bathroom is where he goes to take breaks. The janitor said that when he hangs around outside, people tell him to do things. Zach Braff said that he saw the janitor's penis and noticed a possible melanoma. The janitor asked Zach Braff when he saw his penis. Zach Braff said he saw the janitor's penis while the janitor was taking a shower. The janitor asked Zach Braff where he was when he saw him taking a shower and Zach Braff said that he was outside in the bushes.

'Aubrey is coming over,' Olivia said.

'Tell her I have a UTI and I'm grumpy,' Eric said.

'What?' Olivia said.

'He has a urinary tract infection and he's grumpy,' Sam said.

Eric punched the washing machine. 'I think the washing machine ran out of batteries.'

'Would you guys like me if I was missing my front teeth?' Olivia said.

'No,' Eric said.

'Yes, more,' Jordan said.

'You have all the charm of like, Hilary Swank in *Million Dollar Baby*,' Eric said.

'Which means I have big teeth? Thanks.'

'No,' Eric said. 'Just a lovable bumpkin.'

'I fight people and wear French braids all day,' Olivia said.

'And then Clint Eastwood comes into your life and solves misogyny forever,' Eric said.

'And then I win an Oscar.'

'He's been a vegetarian since the fifties,' Eric said. 'I'm sure he knows what he's talking about.'

'Aubrey will be here soon,' Olivia said. 'I told her you have a UTI.'

'My vagina is gross,' Eric said.

'I heard that men can have UTIs,' Olivia said.

'Have you been listening to me?'

'I don't know. I wouldn't gender you. You're a celestial being.'

Eric stared at Sam. 'Work has changed you,' he said. Sam had just graduated and got a job in his field. 'You come home but I don't feel like you're really home.'

'I am the same,' Sam said.

'Every time someone calls me I want my vision to go blank and I want to hear you say that. Do you think Zach Braff is circumcised?'

'No,' Olivia said.

'Zach Braff has to peel back his foreskin in the shower,' Eric said.

'We should get a Zach Braff poster,' Jordan said.

'I was looking at Zach Braff posters on EBay the other day,' Eric said. 'I need a Zach Braff poster in my bathroom so I can masturbate violently to the Zach Braff poster in my bathroom. Let's get an apartment and have nothing but pictures of Zach Braff.'

'I wonder if they make Zach Braff masks,' Jordan said.

'All you have to do is print out a picture of Zach Braff's face and cut out a tongue hole and you've got a mask,' Eric said.

'Just cut off Zach Braff's face,' Jordan said.

'Oh my God,' Sam said.

'Zach Braff leather,' Eric said.

'I Spent Ninety Days in Jail for Cutting off Zach Braff's Face and It Sucked,' Jordan said.

'I'm going to work for Vice and write a series of articles titled My Life Wearing Zach Braff's Face part one, two, three, four, and five.'

'People treat you a lot different when you're Zach Braff,' Sam said.

'People treat you a lot different when you print out a picture of Zach Braff's face and cut out a tongue hole and put it on your face and walk around Costco without a membership card,' Eric said. 'I want to burn my face off with hot molten lava. Did you know the sun is made out of fire, and that's why I'm going to drive my Kia Rio into it?'

'The sun is actually made out of fusion,' Sam said.

'Just because you graduated doesn't mean you're an expert on the fucking sun,' Eric said.

No one said anything for a minute.

'I'm voting for Ted Cruz,' Eric said. He looked at Jordan. 'Do you wanna run up to Walmart?'

Jordan said sure.

Eric stood and sat on Sam's lap. 'Your butt is warm,' Sam said. 'I like this. Fuck. I forgot Aubrey was coming over. She has a couple of my beers.' He paused and stared at the TV. 'I don't need to drink,' he said in monotone.

'I wish that was my ringtone,' Eric said. 'Going to Walmart for beer three times in one day. Totally normal.'

Jordan and Eric walked outside the apartment. They walked down stairs. Eric opened his car door. He pounded on the seat. Jordan saw a couple roaches crawl under the passenger seat. They got in Eric's car.

'How are your emotions?' Eric said.

'I'm fine.'

'You saw it coming, didn't you?'

'Yeah. I'm surprised I'm like, not that depressed. I thought I would be more depressed.'

'Olivia told me that you're super cute —'

'Oh God,' Jordan said. 'But yeah, I feel okay. I'm gonna stop smoking pot and drinking for a while. I gave my pot to Zach because I owed him thirty dollars for Adderall.'

Eric pulled into the Walmart parking lot. 'Shit,' he said. 'This Walmart only sells alcohol until midnight. We only have fifty-seven minutes.' Jordan and Eric walked inside Walmart. They walked to the beer section and stared at beer. There was a lot of beer. 'This Walmart has an insane beer selection. They have good prices. Fuck. I'm sticking with the champagne of beers. I should buy Colt 45 and black out. Holy shit. A twelve of PBR is eight dollars. An eighteen of Rolling Rock is eleven dollars. This is illegal.'

'Excuse me this is illegal,' Jordan said in a voice. 'Everyone leave.'

'That's a great way to get kicked out of Walmart,' Eric said. 'Fifteen dollars for Busch. They have that Copper Lager, too. I used to love that.'

'Fifteen dollars for the cheapest twenty-four,' Jordan said.

'I'm not getting a twenty-four pack. Leave me alone. I'm the only one drinking. I'm gonna buy a twelve pack of O'Doul's. Maybe that'll make me not a fucking idiot. Pabst is more expensive than Rolling Rock? What kind of topsy-turvy world are we living in?'

'Hell.'

'Should I buy two four-packs of tallboys?'

'If you want an eight pack of tallboys you have no

other choice,' Jordan said.

'You're right,' Eric said. 'Thirty-two-ounce High Life is the same price as a four pack of High Life. I don't want to buy two four packs though.'

'Are you sure?'

'You're a horrible friend.'

'What?'

'I've been doing so good at cutting back. The only real change is self-possessed change. If you don't believe in what you're doing, you're not doing it.'

'Conquer yourself, not the world,' Jordan said.

Eric grabbed two four packs of tallboys. They walked to where mozzarella sticks were. 'I want to be the supreme leader of North Korea and wear a suit made from the breading of mozzarella sticks,' Eric said.

'Breading is breading,' Jordan said. 'It's not specific to certain sticks.'

'What's it like being the voice inside my head?'

'Like a little fairy.'

'I'm sleeping on the couch next to you tonight,' Eric said. He grabbed mozzarella sticks. Jordan and Eric walked to the register. Eric swiped his debit card. 'Yeah it was approved. I'm pretty affluent.'

Jordan and Eric walked outside Walmart. They got in Eric's car. Jordan moved beer cans aside with his foot.

'I'm going to mom-hell,' Eric said. 'It's like regular hell, but it doesn't hurt. It's just sad. Instead of burning alive all you can see is pictures of the faces of everyone you've ever loved looking at you like you just stepped on their toe, like that moment before they recognized that you've just cause them pain. You know what I mean?'

'Are you okay?' Jordan said. He saw a baby in a shopping cart wearing an oversized sweatshirt, eating a banana. 'This is not okay.'

'Kill it,' Eric said. 'This child is staring at me.'

'Kill it,' Jordan said. 'He's wearing a cloak.'

'This kid is going to eat my fucking dreams.'

'This is terrifying.'

'We need to go.'

'He just ate that whole banana.'

*

Jordan and Eric walked inside Eric's apartment. The *Scrubs* theme-song played from the TV.

'Oh shit,' Eric said. He opened a Miller High Life. 'Scrubs is on *and* I'm living the High Life. What a world.'

'Get out of my house,' Sam said.

'I wonder how many people have been elected to leave this apartment,' Olivia said.

'Everybody,' Eric said. 'The only person that hasn't is Jordan.'

'Jordan is much more welcome here than you are,' Sam said. 'Jordan actually pays rent.'

Olivia asked Eric to go outside and smoke with her.

'Don't smoke in my fake leather jacket,' Sam said.

'I'm not.'

'It looks great on you,' Sam said. 'It looks great on everyone because it's a great fucking jacket.'

Jordan, Eric, Olivia, and Aubrey walked outside the apartment. Eric and Olivia lit a cigarette.

'Do you think it's appropriate to list juggling as a skill on your resume?' Aubrey said.

'Depends on where you're applying,' Sam said.

'What the hell,' Eric said while staring at his phone. 'Sam, look at this picture.'

Sam looked at the picture and laughed. Eric showed

Jordan the picture. The picture was of a young man wearing red sunglasses, sitting in a red convertible, smiling like a dumb fucking idiot. 'That's a good car-boy,' Jordan said.

Eric asked Olivia and Aubrey if they wanted to see a real life car-boy.

'Will you send me that?' Jordan said.

Eric said yeah. 'You're still Zach Braff in my phone. Well, your name is ISIS. But your caller ID is a picture of Zach Braff.'

'That's sweet,' Olivia said.

'So whenever Jordan calls me I actually wanna answer for a second.' He showed Jordan a picture of a skeleton saying, 'Let's go ride bikes.'

Jordan stared at the picture for a second. 'That's nice,' he said.

'That's how I felt when I saw it,' Eric said. 'I didn't think it was funny for like thirty seconds.'

'I felt really confused for like two seconds then I felt good.'

'I like the way the bones look, which is unusual for me. I usually hate how bones look.'

'I'm going inside now,' Olivia said. They all walked inside.

'Is this your typewriter?' Aubrey asked Eric.

'Yes,' Eric said. 'I didn't like having to answer that question. I'm going to write my short story for fiction workshop forty times over on the typewriter.'

'All work and no play makes Eric a dull boy,' Sam said.

'I'm gonna rip my legs off,' Eric said. He opened another beer. 'I miss Robert. Robert makes me feel less insane.'

'Really?' Jordan said.

'Yes.'

No one said anything for a minute.

Jordan scrolled through his phone. Eric scrolled through his phone. 'Ricky Calloway burned Mark Zuckerberg,' Eric said. 'He posted on Zuckerberg's picture of his new baby girl and said it was a nice-looking boy.'

'He named his baby Max,' Jordan said.

'Ricky Calloway is an American hero,' Eric said.

'He is my sunshine,' Olivia said.

'I started telling my coworkers that it was okay to get funked sometimes,' Eric said. 'They didn't laugh. They wouldn't look at me. I'm a lone dishwasher.'

'What about the moley-neck girl?' Jordan said.

'None of them thought it was funny.'

'She's funny though.'

'Nope,' Eric said. 'I just clocked out and left.'

'That's always a nice feeling,' Jordan said.

Eric played a Pat the Bunny song on his phone. 'This song reminds me of Robert,' he said.

'Do you wanna eat cigarettes for breakfast tomorrow?' Jordan said.

'I'm gonna have coffee for lunch,' Eric said.

'What are you gonna do for dinner?'

'I'm not that familiar with this song,' Eric said. 'All cops are bastards. Kill every cop you meet.'

Jordan looked at the TV. He read, 'Are you still watching Scrubs?' Jordan said Eric should put that on his tombstone.

'I'm gonna name my daughter the Shins,' Eric said. 'Dawn breaks like a bull through the hall, man. I'm gonna wait until you fall asleep and watch *Garden State*.'

'Can we watch *Garden State* together?' Jordan said.

'It's not on Netflix,' Eric said.

66

'Is it on Hulu?' Aubrey said.

'No,' Eric said.

'That movie makes me too upset,' Eric said. 'It's on my laptop. My laptop is broken.'

'I bought the soundtrack on iTunes,' Aubrey said.

'Fucking millennial,' Eric said. 'The image of Zach Braff putting on headphones and saying, *what is this?* and Natalie Portman saying, *the Shins*. He took a big drink of beer. 'Hamster funeral. Hamster funeral. Hamster funeral. Hamster funeral.'

'Stop,' Jordan said, laughing.

Olivia picked up a small bag. 'What is this?' she said.

'A bag full of cats,' Sam said.

'I'm done with cats,' Jordan said.

Olivia picked up the bag full of cats. 'Why does this exist?'

'I think the best name for a cat is Karen,' Eric said.

'Oh God,' Jordan said. 'That's my manager's name.'

Olivia picked up a cat and showed it to Jordan. 'This is Wilbur,' she said.

'Ugh,' Jordan said. 'Get it away.'

'Don't do that,' Eric said. 'That's fucked up.'

'I'm sorry,' Olivia said.

'I apologize for using derogatory language,' Eric said.

'Why is everyone mean to me tonight?' Olivia said.

'Who is being mean?' Jordan said. 'Sam? Eric?'

'I am guilty of maybe not being so nice,' Eric said.

Olivia closed Netflix and got on YouTube. She played 'Pale Blue Eyes' by the Velvet Underground.

'Can we listen to Smash Mouth?' Sam said.

'I'm going to kill you,' Olivia said, and threw a plastic cat at Sam.

*

A week later Jordan walked inside his house after his night class and saw Ethan watching YouTube videos on the couch, drinking a White Russian. 'We need to get you laid,' Ethan said.

'I don't wanna get laid,' Jordan said. 'I wanna read about the Cold War in my bedroom.' He walked into his room and shut the door. He read about the Cold War.

About an hour later Jordan walked out of his room. The Cold War was depressing him. He saw Sara and another girl drinking White Russians with Ethan. They were watching rap music videos from the 90's. Jordan saw a puppy wearing a vest, running around the house.

'Aw,' Jordan said. 'Whose dog is this?'

'I'm fostering him for the Humane Society,' the girl that wasn't Sara said. She introduced herself to Jordan. Her name was Chelsea. Jordan sat on the couch. Ethan was watching a conspiracy theory video on YouTube about the Earth being flat. 'The astronauts know of the deception, and are sworn to secrecy, under the penalty of whatever motivates them,' the video said.

'Can we watch music videos that are trashy?' Sara said.

Chelsea said yeah.

'I'm so disappointed,' Sara said. 'I found such a good whip-it deal on the Internet, but they're out of stock.'

Chelsea hummed a song and asked what the name of the song was.

'I know what you're humming I just can't think of the name.'

Chelsea looked at Jordan. 'What's that song?'

'I have no idea.'

She hummed again. 'Wait, now I'm humming a

different song.'

Jordan stared at Ethan. He was making a face and staring at his phone.

'Free shipping,' Sara said. 'Twenty-one dollars for sixty whip-its.'

Jordan asked Ethan if the world was flat. Ethan said he watched the whole twelve minute video and felt convinced that the world was flat. 'Have you ever seen a shot of an astronaut where the earth wasn't in the background?' Ethan said. 'And why doesn't the international space station have any windows facing space?'

'They do have pictures of space,' Chelsea said.

'Prove it,' Ethan said. 'Show me an astronaut and space behind him.'

Jordan asked how that would prove the Earth is flat.

'There's a dome over the earth,' Ethan said. 'People are watching us do shit.' He looked up at the TV and said the music video wasn't slutty enough, and that the woman in the video was too empowered.

Chelsea said the woman in the video was working it.

'She is the baddest bitch,' Sara said.

'Doesn't matter,' Ethan said. 'Why isn't she slutty? I thought we were going to watch terrible slutty videos. Put on 'That's That' by R. Kelly.'

Chelsea said that Sara gets to pick the next video then Jordan then Ethan.

Ethan poured himself another White Russian. 'Would you like one, Jordan?'

Jordan said sure.

Sara told Ethan to save her some. She played the song 'I Ain't Got No Panties On' by Wax-A-Million. Chelsea gave Jordan the controller and he played the music video for 'Best Friend' by Young Thug. In the video Young Thug and his friends did things in the woods together while wearing expensive clothing.

'Those are his best friends and they're having a great time together,' Sara said.

Jordan said that he likes when Young Thug calls his friends lovers.

'Maybe they have sex,' Sara said. 'No, probably not.'

'Lovers and friends,' Chelsea said.

'I know what I'm going to play for my turn,' Sara said. 'I'm so excited. Do you have shot glasses? I'm pretty sure the puppy pissed on your jacket, Ethan.'

Ethan picked up his jacket. 'Yeah,' he said. 'At least he's a tiny-ass puppy.'

'He doesn't like you,' Jordan said. He picked up the puppy. 'Your eyes are really far apart.'

'He's really young,' Chelsea said. 'So like, his face hasn't grown into his eyes. He does look stupid right now.'

'You look stupid,' Jordan said to the puppy.

'He looks a little special,' Chelsea said in a funny voice.

Sara walked into the kitchen and opened the fridge. She walked into the living room holding a large bottle of Kirkland Vodka.

'Top-shelf Kirkland,' Jordan said. He thought about the time he and Emma drank screwdrivers in his dorm and then put the vodka in the freezer and the next day it was frozen.

'I put that shit in the freezer one time and it froze,' he said.

'Really?' Chelsea said.

Jordan said yeah.

'Maybe that's why I didn't feel drunk after that ginormous mixed drink.'

They all took a shot of Kirkland Vodka.

Chelsea played a Big Freedia video where Big Freedia and other women shook their asses very fast in different locations. Jordan said that he saw Big Freedia at a music festival. Chelsea said that she went to the music festival Jordan was talking about. Jordan said that he accidentally smoked opium at 4 a.m. during Big Freedia's set.

Jordan looked at Ethan and said Ethan's mouth was wide open while watching the video. Ethan closed his mouth.

Sara played the music video for the song 'I love you' by Lil B. Lil B held large snakes for most of the video and then cried near the end and said sometimes things get real shiesty and that he loved everyone and that the world was big and he wanted to spread love and that he was crying for everyone.

Ethan played a Das Racist video for a song called 'Manny Pacquiao' where people danced with guns and chickens on a farm.

Jordan played 'Dust in a Gold Sack' by the band Swearin' and Chelsea said Swearin' was one of her favorite bands.

A little later Sara asked Chelsea if she was ready to leave. Chelsea said she was going to stay a little while longer. Sara left and ten minutes later Ethan took a swig of vodka and said he was going to bed. Jordan and Chelsea sat on the couch and watched more music videos. Jordan felt drunk. He said he was tired. Chelsea said she was tired too, but didn't feel like walking home. 'You can sleep on the couch if you want,' Jordan said. Chelsea didn't say anything. She smiled at Jordan. 'Or you can sleep in my bed.'

'That sounds good,' Chelsea said. They lay together

on a twin-mattress on the floor of Jordan's room and fell asleep.

*

A few days later Jordan stood at the Starbucks on campus, waiting for his iced coffee. He saw Olivia waiting for coffee, too. He went and stood next to Olivia.

'What are you doing tonight?' he said.

'I don't know,' Olivia said. 'I've been depressed.'

Jordan said he was sorry that she felt depressed.

'Do you want to drink Malt Liquor with me?' Olivia said.

'Yeah,' Jordan said. 'Wanna drink in the park?'

*

At the park Jordan and Olivia drank malt-liquor on a bench by a small pond and looked at ducks. They talked about writing. Olivia talked about a short story she was writing about Ted Cruz and the Zika Virus. Jordan felt happy to be drinking beer outside. He saw a cop walk toward them. He pushed the beer under the bench with his foot.

'Have you guys seen an old man walking around?' the cop said. 'He escaped from the nursing home.'

'No,' they both said. The cop walked away.

'Jacksonville cops are really stupid,' Jordan said.

*

They finished the beers and drove back to Jordan's house. They smoked marijuana on the couch and watched a kung-fu movie starring Jackie Chan. Ethan,

Daniel, Chelsea, and Abby walked inside the house. Jordan felt drunk and stoned. He stood and walked toward Ethan and said he needed to talk to him. They went into Ethan's room.

'What am I doing?' Jordan said. 'I mean, what should I do?'

'About what?'

'They're both here. Olivia and Chelsea. I don't like Olivia. I mean, she's my friend. I might like Chelsea.'

'I don't know, man. Relax. Act normal.'

*

Everyone sat on the couch and watched the kung-fu movie. About an hour later Chelsea left. Olivia asked Jordan if he wanted to go to his bed. Jordan said okay. They went into Jordan's bedroom and had sex. They lay in bed for twenty minutes then Olivia gave Jordan a blow-job and he came in her mouth. 'I thought you were going to penetrate again,' Olivia said.

'Oh,' Jordan said.

*

'Dude,' Robert texted Jordan the next afternoon.

'What?' Jordan said.

'I just inherited 30,000 dollars.'

'Shit,' Jordan said.

'Yeah man.'

'Seriously?'

'Yeah. Don't tell anyone. I had to tell someone.'

'Sugar daddy,' Jordan said. 'Buy a yacht.'

'Maybe a motorcycle. I feel strange with this much power. I'm like a one-percenter.'

'You are Jeff Bezos,' Jordan said.

'Should I buy a van? Or a trailer in Canada? Dude. What do I do? Did I tell you I think I'm in love?'

'Probably invest. Really? Who is it?'

'Some girl I've been sleeping with in Baltimore. She goes to art school.'

'Nice. Your life is awesome now.'

'I miss Jacksonville.'

'I miss you.'

'Fuck Jacksonville actually. I miss you and Eric though.'

'I've gotta go to work,' Jordan texted. 'Don't blow all your money on beer.'

*

On February 4th, Eric texted Jordan, 'I am very sad. Would you want to exist in the same room as me this weekend? Soon, I mean. I am very sad. I'm listening to Tech N9ne in the rain. I'm so fucked.'

'Yeah. Why are you sad?'

'I am fucked. I wish I was president. Presidents can go look at aliens when they are sad. I want to see an alien.'

'Chelsea is having a party tonight if you wanna come.'

'That might be good. What kind of party?'

'Just a party,' Jordan said.

*

'I'm telling Kim that I don't want to talk to her tonight,' Eric said about an hour later while sitting next to Jordan on the couch in Jordan's living room.

'She's going to be upset.'

'Why are you saying that?' Eric said. 'You're so fucked. Should I leave and drive across town and go talk to her?'

'I thought you meant you don't want to text her.'

'She wanted me to come over and talk after she got off work.'

'Don't do that.'

Daniel and Abby walked into the living room. Jordan introduced them to Eric. Daniel asked what food he should go eat. Jordan said that the Mexican place that just opened up down the road was good.

Daniel said thanks and he and Abby walked outside the house.

'There they go,' Eric said. 'Out of my life forever.'

Jordan said Daniel and Abby were coming to the party.

Eric said he was going to kill himself at the party. He said they should go to the corner store and buy beer. Jordan said they should buy beer and drink at the house for like an hour then drive to the party. Eric said he would drive. 'I'm going to bring my hammer to the corner store,' Eric said while staring at his phone. 'Kim isn't happy. You were right. She asked what time I wanted to talk tomorrow. Apparently she didn't want to break up with me, but this morning she said we should talk, which I assumed meant breaking up.'

'That is what that means. Emma said that to me and then broke up with me.'

'To communicate her sadness she posted a photo of an Amy Winehouse vinyl on Instagram,' Eric said. 'Fucking kill me.'

*

They drove to the corner store. Jordan bought a twelve pack of beer and a Lil Wayne mixtape. They drove with the windows down and listened to Lil Wayne and drank beer.

'Olivia said that Ethan was really mean to you the other night.'

'I don't know,' Jordan said. 'I was just high. I think everyone is being mean when I'm stoned.'

'Olivia said he was being mean.'

'She was probably high too. She texted me tonight.'

'She wants to do it again, and I told her, *let Jordan be Jordan*.'

'Uh, do what again?'

'She wants to like, see you, or something.'

'It's my fault,' Jordan said. 'I had to drive her back to the dorms the next morning and I was hungover as shit. Olivia is my friend. Why did we do that?'

'I was very uncomfortable.'

'I did that. That was me. I'm a bad, bad man.'

'Stop,' Eric said. 'I'm trying to be sad right now. I'm going to fuck Ethan tonight.'

'Fuck him,' Jordan said. 'He's having relationship problems. As we all are.'

'Fuck off.'

'Actually, I'm not anymore,' Jordan said. 'Wow. I'm glad that's over.'

'Stop,' Eric said. 'I don't wanna talk about it.'

'Breaking up with your girlfriend is awesome. Or, getting broken up with is awesome.'

'I don't wanna think about it tonight. Tomorrow is going to suck.'

'I think it'll work out.'

'Yeah, I'm sure. I'm a stupid fucking monkey. People are just monkeys with nukes.'

'Everyone is a stupid little monkey.'

'Some monkeys are just dumber than others.'

'We have to remember not to talk like this in front of everyone,' Jordan said.

'I was doing this last night at the bar and they weren't happy about it.'

'I love thinking about people as being monkeys.'

'Aubrey was giving me a ride home from the bar and I kept saying, *look at my little monkey fingers*.'

'Whoever we elect is going to be a monkey,' Jordan said. 'Which monkey is going to be in charge of America?'

'Jeb,' Eric said. 'He eats yogurt with his fingers.' Jordan wrote a short story about Jeb Bush eating yogurt with his fingers and showed it to Eric during their fiction workshop class.

'It all sounds so harmless.'

'Jeb sounds harmless. He just wants everyone to like him.'

'He eats yogurt with his fingers,' Eric said. 'Did you kiss Chelsea yet?'

'Last night I did.'

'Did you kiss her real hard on the face?'

'I think so. I was very drunk. I keep getting very drunk.'

'You won't get drunk with me, but you'll get trashed with her. I'm so upset.'

'I've been drunk four times this week. I can't believe she doesn't think I'm an idiot. She's gotten drunk too, I guess. I wish Robert was here. Fuck. I wish Robert was here.'

*

Jordan and Eric pulled up to the address Chelsea sent him. It was Tom's house. Chelsea and Tom lived together. Jordan and Eric walked inside and sat on a couch and drank beer. They played a drinking game, sat on the porch, shotgunned a couple beers, listened to Daniel and Abby argue. Eventually everyone left and Jordan and Chelsea went into her room. Chelsea touched Jordan's penis.

'I don't have any condoms,' Jordan said.

'I have a lot of condoms,' Chelsea said. 'Tom got me a piñata full of condoms for my birthday.'

'Wow,' Jordan said, and they had sex.

*

Jordan woke up at 7:30 a.m. He was still drunk. Chelsea drove Jordan back to his house. Jordan put on a chef coat and drove to work. At work the manager told Jordan he had to train two new food-runners. Every time Jordan showed up drunk to work it seemed like he had to train someone. One of the new food-runners was named Zolton. He was a high school kid that had just quit his job at Taco Bell.

'I was up all night playing Xbox,' Zolton said. 'I was just like, fuck it.' He said something in a Hispanic accent, and then said something else in an Arnold Schwarzenegger accent. 'These are things you learn when you play Xbox. The Schwarzenegger accent took me like a year, but the cholo accent, I got it just like, immediately.'

'Okay,' Jordan said.

The other new food-runner was named Torian. He told Jordan he had just been fired from the Hooters across the river. He said that he was trying to be a rapper. Torian picked up a tray and his braids lay in a pool of gravy next to some meatloaf.

'My braids keep lying in the juice,' he said.

Zolton smelled a latex glove and said the glove smelled like a condom. He told Jordan to smell the glove. Jordan said that he didn't want to smell the glove. 'Just smell the glove,' Zolton said. 'They smell like condoms.'

Jordan smelled a glove. He said it smelled like a condom.

'At Taco Bell I put mayonnaise on crackers as a snack,' Zolton said.

Jordan didn't say anything.

Zolton moved really close to Jordan. 'Put mayonnaise on a cracker and eat it,' Zolton said, almost whispering.

'I don't want to do that.'

'Put mayonnaise on a cracker and eat it because it's fucking good.'

'I don't want to.'

Zolton put mayonnaise on a saltine cracker and handed it to Jordan.

Jordan stared at the cracker. 'I don't want to eat this,' he said.

Zolton stared at Jordan.

Jordan ate the mayonnaise cracker.

'Fuckin good, right?'

'It tastes like a saltine cracker with mayonnaise.'

'Hell yeah,' Zolton said. 'Condiments are awesome.' Zolton walked away. He filled a Styrofoam cup with coffee. He carved his name into the Styrofoam cup with a soup spoon.

'Fucking psychopath,' Jordan thought. He was expediting food. The heat lamp was hot on his face and he thought he might puke. Zolton moved close to Jordan again.

'Do you wanna go to a cars and coffee festival with me?' Zolton said. 'It's under a bridge.'

'What?'

'Cars and coffee.'

'I don't what you're saying.'

'Cars and coffee festival. Under a bridge. Do you wanna go?'

'What?' Jordan said. 'No.'

*

Jordan clocked out a few hours later. He drove home and lay on the couch and ate a PB&J taco. 'Guess what I found the puppy chewing on?' Chelsea texted Jordan.

'Oh no,' Jordan texted. 'Not the condom.'

'Bingo.'

'We've tainted him. The Humane Society is going to arrest us. They will ask why their puppy is full of condoms.'

'He's going to poop condoms forever.'

'He needs guidance.'

Jordan could hear Ethan having sex.

'Ethan is fucking really loud,' he texted Chelsea. 'This is bad.'

'How loud?'

'Too loud.'

'With his girlfriend? Or a mistress?'

'His girlfriend, I think.'

'Is she loud?'

'She is even louder.'

'I've never heard my roommates have sex.'

'That's good. What're you up too?'

'Watching anime with the puppy. What about you?'

'Eating a taco on the couch. Do you wanna hang out at your place?'

*

At Chelsea's house they played with the puppy. They smoked marijuana out of a disgusting gravity bong. They lay in Chelsea's bed. They kissed for a couple minutes. Chelsea said she was on her period.

'That's okay,' Jordan said. They kissed more. Jordan lay on his back and stared the ceiling. Chelsea rubbed Jordan's stomach then put her hand in his pants and touched his penis. She gave Jordan a blowjob and they fell asleep.

*

A few days later Jordan and Chelsea watched *Hail Caesar*, the new Coen brothers movie, at Sunray, a small theatre where Chelsea worked as a cashier. After the movie they drove to Chelsea's house. Chelsea said that she took the puppy back to the Humane Society earlier, but had kittens and a momma cat now. They played with the kittens. They smoked marijuana out of the gravity bong. They lay in bed and watched *Watership Down* on Chelsea's computer then slept.

*

'Does this kitten look okay?' Chelsea said in the morning.

Jordan got out of bed and looked at the kitten. The kitten was flattened. It was dead.

'I think it's dead,' Jordan said. They stared at the dead kitten.

'The momma cat crushed her,' Chelsea said. She put the dead kitten in a shoe-box. She called the Humane Society. She asked them what she should do with the dead kitten. The Humane Society told Chelsea it didn't matter. Chelsea hung up the phone. She asked Jordan if he wanted to go to a vegan bakery and eat donuts.

*

At the bakery they sat inside on a small couch and ate donuts and drank coffee. The donut was fucking delicious. Jordan didn't understand how a vegan donut could taste so good. Jordan saw kids looking through a mail slot in the door. 'I'm going to pour hot coffee on their face,' Jordan said. He thought maybe he didn't know Chelsea well enough to be saying insane bullshit yet.

'We should slide the dead cat through the slot,' Chelsea said. 'The Humane Society said it doesn't matter. That lady was a fucking nihilist.'

'I feel bad for the dead kitten,' Jordan said.

'It's dead,' Chelsea said. 'There's nothing we can do.'

Jordan thought about the ending to *A Farewell to Arms*. They made plans to hangout the next day. Jordan didn't realize that the next day was Valentine's Day. He remembered that Robert was coming home.

*

On Valentine's Day Jordan woke around 7:45 a.m. He drove to work. He tried to avoid eye contact with Emma, but sometimes looked at Emma.

82

Around 2 p.m. he sat in the bathroom and texted Chelsea, 'I think I'm getting sick. Can we hangout another night?'

'Oh no,' Chelsea texted. 'That sucks. But yeah, rain check is fine. I'm sorry you probably caught my cold.'

After work Jordan drove to a co-worker's house and bought marijuana. He went to the gym. He drove home and read a nonfiction book about how fucked the world was. Robert texted Jordan and asked if he wanted to meet him at a party at Aubrey's. Jordan said he did. He picked up his car keys and walked outside his bedroom. Someone knocked on the door and Ethan answered the door. It was Chelsea. Jordan put his keys inside his pocket and sat on the couch. Chelsea sat on the couch next to Jordan. They watched Ethan play Fallout New Vegas. Jordan felt annoyed that Chelsea came over after he said he was sick. He didn't want to say he was going to a party without her. He said he was feeling better and asked Chelsea if she wanted to go to a party. Chelsea said that she did. She grabbed Jordan's face and squeezed it. She asked if he was scared. 'No,' he said.

'You guys are so cute together,' Ethan said.

Daniel walked into the living room. He asked Ethan if he was doing anything for Valentine's Day. Ethan said that his girlfriend was asleep and that he was going to play video games all night. Daniel said Abby's friends were in town from Miami and that they made a feast.

Chelsea asked what Jordan's friend's name was.

'Robert,' Jordan said. 'But we call him GG Allin sometimes. Or just GG I mean.'

*

Jordan and Chelsea drove in Jordan's car. They stopped

by the corner store and bought a twelve pack. They listened to Waxahatchee and drove with the windows down. Jordan thought about open-containering, but didn't, because he wasn't sure how Chelsea would feel about it. 'I need a new job,' Jordan said. 'I don't want to work with my ex-girlfriend. I make a lot of money though, for what I do. I made sixteen dollars an hour last night.'

'Just for carrying food around?' Chelsea said.

'Yeah,' Jordan said.

*

At Aubrey's house everyone was sitting outside in lawn chairs, drinking beer and smoking marijuana. Jordan gave Robert a hug. He introduced Chelsea to Robert.

'Did you end up going to New York?' Jordan said.

'No. I went to Baltimore, Ohio, and West Virginia. People in West Virginia are assholes. No one would give me money. I need to get a job. I found out that my uncle is the number one goldfish breeder in America.'

'That's good,' Jordan said. A dog walked toward Jordan and put his paws on Jordan's chest.

Jordan said the dog was good.

'I saw a dog at the Humane Society that was half-pug, half-pomeranian,' Chelsea said. 'It was old and fat and had patchy long hair. I wanted to adopt him. No one else will.'

'Aren't pugs like, retarded?' Robert said. 'Like, they weren't meant to exist?'

'I think so,' Chelsea said. 'But they're so cute.'

'You're looking crusty,' Jordan said to Robert. 'The rat-tail is long.'

'I'm a trust fund punk,' Robert said. 'I don't have to

work. I'm gonna lie on the floor and drink PBR and not go to school.'

'That's awesome,' Jordan said.

'I'll get depressed. Last night I drank expensive rum from South America that tasted like Christmas tree and slept on my friend's pull out couch. I need to get a job. I don't wanna work at Winn-Dixie. I'm not good at talking to people.'

'You can have my job,' Aubrey said. 'I'm quitting.'

'It's probably not a good job,' Robert said. 'Since you're quitting.'

'You're right. It sucks.'

Sam parked his car and walked toward the house.

'What's up?' Jordan said. 'This is Chelsea.'

'Hi,' Sam said, and gave Jordan a hug, then gave Chelsea a hug.

'Did you graduate?' Robert said to Sam.

'Yeah,' Sam said. He looked at the dog. 'Whose dog?'

'That's Doug,' Aubrey said. 'We found him outside the Murphy's Express. We're keeping him.'

'He looks so happy,' Sam said.

'We took him to beach earlier and he chased seagulls,' Aubrey said.

'Was it cold the whole time?' Jordan asked Robert.

'Negative two degrees.'

'Did you sleep in your car?'

'A few times.'

'I'm glad you're back.'

'Me too,' Robert said. 'I was going crazy for a little while.'

Jordan took marijuana out of his pocket and asked Aubrey to use her bong. Jordan, Chelsea, and Aubrey smoked marijuana. They walked inside, sat around the dolphin table.

'How's your job?' Jordan asked Sam.

'Good,' Sam said. 'I get to draw roads all day.'

Robert handed Jordan a raspberry Shock Top.

'Motherfucker,' Jordan said. 'What is this shit?'

'I stole it from my dad's mini-fridge.'

'You're fucked,' Jordan said. He held the bong toward Robert. 'Do you want some?'

'I smoked pot last night and threw up.'

'I threw up because of dabs the other night,' Chelsea said.

'I used to smoke dabs and get way too high for like two minutes then feel okay,' Sam said.

'I like dabs,' Chelsea said.

'Zach used to smoke dabs like ten times a day,' Jordan said. He took a sip of the raspberry beer. 'This beer is strange.'

'I really feel like stealing some Colt 45,' Robert said.

'We can,' Jordan said. 'There are Walmarts all over the world.'

'How was working with Emma on Valentine's Day?' Robert said.

'Fucking weird,' Jordan said. He sat back in his chair. He felt stoned. He looked at Chelsea while she talked to Aubrey. Emma was never very social around his friends. Chelsea seemed more social.

'Have you hungout with Zach lately?' Robert said.

'We walked around San Marco the day after me and Emma broke up.'

'That's nice,' Robert said.

Sam said something about Xanax.

'That's fucked,' Robert said.

Jordan said he was glad that Robert was back because he always says when things are fucked and he doesn't know when something is fucked when Robert isn't around.

Sam picked up a funny looking hat. He put the hat on his head.

'That's fucked,' Robert said.

'You look like you should be walking a small dog,' Jordan said.

'Someone take a picture,' Sam said. Jordan took a picture of Sam and showed Sam the picture. Sam laughed.

'You should spend thirty grand on cocaine and sell thirty grand worth of cocaine,' Jordan said.

'I've thought about it,' Robert said. 'I could double my money.'

'Do you think Robert should sell cocaine?' Jordan asked Chelsea.

Chelsea said yeah.

'Will you buy some?' Robert said.

'A small amount,' Chelsea said. 'Cocaine has never really done anything for me.'

'You haven't tried Robert's coke though,' Jordan said.

'You should buy a houseboat,' Chelsea said.

'I met a girl that lived on a houseboat while I was on the road.'

'Art school girl?' Jordan said.

'No.'

'What was up with her?'

'I stayed with her for like a week. She was an RA. We'd wake up and go to the dining hall and eat and then I'd lay in her bed while she was in class. She's mad at me because I left after I found out she wasn't pregnant. I'm never not wearing a condom again.'

'Have you seen Eric yet?' Jordan said.

'No. What's he doing tonight?'

'He's probably with Kim.'

'I wanna get drunk with some Juggalos,' Robert said. 'I met a Juggalo on the internet on this traveling kids website and hung out with him, then found out that he was a child molester.'

'That's not good,' Jordan said. 'It's good to see you. You were gone for a long time. I missed you.'

'A lot of shit has changed since I've been gone,' Robert said. 'Your life is different.'

'Yeah,' Jordan said. 'Like, quickly. Yeah.'

Sam walked up to Jordan and Robert. Robert looked at Sam. 'Did you know Marlon Brando is dead? I just found out he died in like, 2004,' Robert said.

'I thought you were going to say he died this week or something,' Jordan said.

'We need to get high and watch *the Godfather*,' Robert said.

'Do you have class in the morning?'

'No. We should get breakfast. Do you have class?'

'I'm not in school.'

'Oh yeah.'

'When I was in Baltimore I stayed in my cousin's house, and they had upstairs neighbors that were loud as shit, and it made me realize that we were probably loud as shit in your old apartment, when I was living in the closet. I miss that trashed-ass place.'

'That place was fucking trashed,' Jordan said.

'No one did anything. Once a week we'd get hopped up on caffeine and amphetamines and clean the house.'

'God, man,' Jordan said. 'That was a strange living situation. That would still be happening if we didn't get kicked out. God, I'd be miserable. I'd be miserable and fat. I would.'

'I'm glad I don't have to deal with that cat anymore,'

Robert said. 'Have you seen it since?'

'No. I'll never see it again.'

'I'll kick that cat in the face.'

'I liked Wilbur.'

'I have nightmares about those fleas,' Robert said. When Robert lived in the closet they had a flea infestation. 'I lived in a flea infested storage closet. I remember one night when I came home trashed and the fleas wouldn't stop biting me so I slept in my car.'

'You lived in a flea infested closet,' Jordan said, laughing.

'I had a TV in there though, and a PlayStation.'

'I miss that shit, man,' Jordan said. 'That was awesome when you lived with us.'

Robert laughed a little. 'That was fun, man.'

Jordan laughed a little. 'You used to put that dress on and we'd go to Rain Dogs —'

'Aw man, I miss that dress.'

'— And sit outside. We can still do that. Yeah. We can still do that.'

'Can we still hang out at the spot one night?' Robert said. The spot was an empty storefront next to Rain Dogs. Crust punks with guitars and pit bulls would always hangout out front.

'It's so weird how things from that recent are like, shit, that you like, talk about —'

'I know.'

'— As like, things that happened like, a long time ago. That's how I feel when I think about old apartments.'

'That's like, ancient history. Going over there. Grilling hot dogs in like, the front yard, or wherever. On that shitty-ass little grill. Every place we've lived, or that you've lived, I feel like the neighbors have thought that your friends were just fucked.'

'We were fucked.'

*

Around 9 p.m. a couple weeks later Jordan and Chelsea sat on her couch.

'Do you want to do whip-its and watch *Beavis and Butthead*?' Chelsea said.

'Sure.' Chelsea opened her computer. She played *Beavis and Butthead*.

Chelsea had gotten a new dog about a week ago. It jumped onto the couch and stared at Chelsea while she opened a box of whip-its. 'She's giving disapproving glances,' Jordan said.

'She's like, that one commercial with the dog that's like, *I don't like when you smoke weed*.'

Jordan looked at the dog. 'I don't care what you think.' He watched Chelsea do a whip-it. 'I can never get the whole whip-it in one breath.'

Jordan said he was at a party in high school once and saw someone do three at the same time. He said he was excited to do LSD in Georgia. Jordan, Chelsea, Daniel, and Abby were going camping at a canyon created from bad farming practices in Georgia over spring break. Chelsea said she hoped the weather was nice.

Jordan looked at Beavis and Butthead. A teacher was mad at Beavis and Butthead for laughing during attendance. The teacher told Beavis and Butthead that they weren't allowed to laugh for a week or they'll get expelled.

Chelsea held up the box of whippets. 'Do you want to do one or two?'

'One.' Jordan did a whip-it.

Tom walked inside the apartment.

'Hi Tommy,' Chelsea said.

'Are you whipping?' Tom said, smiling.

'I'm whipping.'

'I saved some,' Tom said. 'And there's some in the couch.'

'What?'

'I stored one in the couch so you wouldn't do it. I wanted to do one more before I go to bed. One more good one.' Tom sat on the couch.

Jordan looked at Beavis and Butthead. Beavis spray-painted *Megadeth* on a house. Butthead lit a bush on fire and drove away on a riding lawnmower.

Tom loaded up three whip-it canisters.

'Don't do so many that you suffocate, Tommy,' Chelsea said. Jordan didn't like when Chelsea called Tom that.

'I'm not,' Tom said. He did three whip-its. He stared at the computer and made noises that Jordan thought sounded like Beavis and Butthead laughing but lower-pitched.

'Shut up,' Chelsea said.

'Sorry,' Tom said a few seconds later. 'I've never done whip-its before today. Can you stand up so I can get the whip-its under your ass?'

'Don't say ass,' Chelsea said.

'I like saying ass.' Chelsea stood and Tom looked at the couch. 'I think one fell down,' he said.

'Yeah it did,' Chelsea said. 'I heard it.'

*

'Would you like some LSD with your coffee?' Chelsea said, smiling. It was March 15th. They were in Georgia, sitting at a picnic table near their campsite. Chelsea was dressed in an American flag bathing suit.

'I guess so,' Jordan said. He felt hungover.

Ten minutes later, after finishing his coffee and ingesting LSD, Jordan went and threw up a little in the grass, about twenty feet from the campsite, and began to feel gradually less nauseous, over the next thirty minutes, until he felt okay enough to ride in a car.

Jordan and Chelsea sat in the backseat of her car. Daniel drove and Abby sat in the passenger seat. Chelsea looked at Jordan. She smiled. 'I just want you to have a great day,' she said. Jordan felt nauseous again.

*

They got out of the car and walked toward the entrance to the canyon.

Daniel started talking to an old man with yellow teeth. 'I'm here because I'm a creationist,' the man said.

'I think, uh, this canyon is man-made. From bad irrigation practices,' Daniel said.

The man made a face. 'That's a conspiracy,' he said. The man's cell phone started ringing.

Jordan walked quickly into the bathroom near the entrance of the canyon. He stood at the urinal. He stared at the wall and it seemed to be moving a little. He looked in the mirror then remembered that someone told him not to look at mirrors while on acid and he walked outside the bathroom. The creationist man was gone.

*

They walked down a shaded path. Jordan was starting

to feel the acid. 'These lizards are everywhere,' Jordan said. 'They're so fat.'

'You're seeing lizards?' Abby said.

'Yeah,' Jordan said, and pointed at a lizard on a tree. 'There's one.'

'Oh, I thought you meant you were hallucinating them,' Abby said and laughed.

'Oh yeah,' Jordan said. 'I am. All of you look like giant lizards.' Abby and Daniel were sober. Jordan felt weird about being on LSD around people that weren't on LSD.

'Thank you Jesus for creating these giant lizards that are nice to look at,' Jordan said. He felt unexpectedly sarcastic. 'That's the most profound thing I'm going to say while on acid.' He watched Chelsea's dog try to eat a butterfly. He felt impressed by the dog's level of concentration.

Chelsea grabbed Jordan's hand. 'How do you feel?' she said.

'I feel good,' Jordan said. He didn't want to talk to Chelsea. 'How do you feel?'

'I feel like, overwhelmed. Just a lot of emotions. And on top of everything else that has been happening like, between us.'

Jordan stared at the ground. He let go of Chelsea's hand.

'You can't describe the feeling at all?' Chelsea said.

'I just like being outside.' He walked and stood near the edge of the canyon with Daniel, and thought, 'This is my experience. I don't have to share it with anyone,' in regards to his acid trip, and also life in general. He felt extremely aware that his experience, as a person on Earth, would be unlike anyone else's experience ever, and felt good about the rest of his life. He also thought that Chelsea, Daniel, and Abby were not the right people to have taken acid with for the first time, since he barely really knew any of them, and felt like he wanted to call Eric or Robert, but couldn't, because his phone was dead. He decided to accept everything that might happen, and focus on keeping to himself, and seeming like he wasn't on acid.

'Myra isn't drinking water,' Chelsea said a few minutes later. Myra was the dog's name. 'I think she might have rabies.'

'She definitely has rabies,' Jordan said, annoyed that Chelsea was talking to him.

*

Jordan and Daniel climbed rocks and stood near the top of the canyon. Jordan heard Chelsea yell 'be careful,' and Jordan yelled back, 'I have a lot of control on acid,' and a touristy looking coupled stared at him. Jordan said the canyon was beautiful.

*

A few hours later they ate food at a Mardi Gras themed restaurant, then bought 40-ounces of Colt 45 at a convenience store that sold porno DVDs.

Later that night, after drinking a 40-ounce of Colt 45 around the fire with Chelsea, Daniel, and Abby, Jordan walked away from the campsite, and looked up at the stars while peeing. He thought, 'I'm experiencing the world. I'm young. This is good.' He got inside the tent with Chelsea and played a Nana Grizol song on his phone. He thought about ending his relationship with Chelsea, but also thought that he should try to enjoy the next two days, and not seem openly disinterested in continuing their relationship. He thought that he didn't want to lead her on anymore, then rolled over on his side and kissed her forehead spontaneously, and she kissed him on the mouth.

'Do you have one?' she said.

'Um, I think so. I mean, yeah. I have one.'

'You do have one?'

'Yeah,' Jordan said, and they had sex, then he fell asleep facing away from Chelsea.

*

The next morning they got in Chelsea's car and drove toward a place called Snooki's diner. Chelsea kept changing the song on her phone. She swerved off the road a little. Jordan and Daniel were in the back seat together. Daniel looked at Jordan. Chelsea changed the song again and swerved off the road. Daniel leaned forward and grabbed the phone out of Chelsea's hand. 'You're being a retard,' he yelled.

'Don't grab phones out of people's hands,' Abby said.

'Do you want to die?' Daniel said. 'She's going to kill us.'

*

Outside the diner, Chelsea started crying and said she would be inside soon. Jordan walked inside and ordered fried chicken, macaroni and cheese, and collard greens. He sat at the table with Daniel and they ate without talking. Chelsea came inside and sat at the table and said she had an anxiety attack. Jordan noticed that her eyes were watery. He thought, 'I don't want to deal with another person's emotions right now,' and stared at his food. Chelsea went into the bathroom and Abby followed.

*

Back at the campsite Daniel was packing his things. Abby had to be back in Jacksonville that night. Daniel and Abby left. Jordan sat at a picnic table with Chelsea.

'Do you want to go on a hike or something?' Chelsea said.

'Do you want to stay another night?' Jordan said. 'I kind of want to go home. I haven't seen my parents in a while and I don't wanna sleep in a tent again.'

'You want to leave?'

'Yeah. Kind of. Yeah...I want to leave.'

Jordan lay down on the picnic table and stared at the sky, not feeling like making eye contact with Chelsea because he thought she might cry.

'So you're going back to St. Augustine?' Chelsea said.

'Yeah. I haven't seen my parents in a while.'

Chelsea said okay.

Neither of them said anything for a minute.

'Do you think anything about us?' Chelsea said, and laughed nervously.

'I don't know. I just, kind of feel like, um, I was just like, dating Emma for so long, and I feel like I probably need to be single for a while.'

'Yeah,' Chelsea said. 'I kind of thought that. I just wanted to ask.'

'But I like, like hanging out with you.'

'Yeah,' Chelsea said. 'I like what we're doing right now. I'm fine with it. Sorry if that was awkward.' She started crying a little.

'I should have said something sooner,' Jordan said.

*

On the drive home Jordan played *The Life of Pablo*. He stopped at Subway and bought a veggie sub for Chelsea and one for himself. He bought a 40-ounce of Colt 45 for Robert and Eric.

*

A few days later Jordan texted Eric a picture of himself smoking marijuana in bed. 'I'm too high,' Jordan texted.

Eric sent Jordan a picture of himself holding a 40-ounce of Colt 45. He texted, 'Call the cops. Aren't you sober and superior?' After Jordan came back from the camping trip he told Eric he was going to be sober for a while and read books in his room.

'I'm John Updike and I'm high on K2,' Jordan texted.

'I'm Norman Mailer and I smoke crack.'

'Eric,' Jordan texted. 'What am I supposed to do with my time on Earth?'

'Read books and do nitrous,' Eric texted. 'Send me pictures of books that engage you on your isolationist odyssey.'

Jordan sent Eric a picture from the book *Matt Meets Vik* by Timothy Willis Sanders. 'What the fuck are you reading?' Eric said. 'Alternative literature?'

*

A couple months later, on June 30th, Jordan and Abby sat outside Rain Dogs and drank beer. He had read a lot of books and smoked a lot of marijuana alone in his room over the last couple months and wanted to be social again. Abby had broken up with Daniel, and Daniel was going to be gone for two months. He was in Bloomington, Indiana working at a sculpture park. Jordan and Abby walked across the street to Wall Street, a dive bar in Five Points, and took tequila shots and drank beer. Abby said she wanted to get stoned. Jordan said he wanted to get stoned too. They got in Abby's car and drove toward Jordan's house. They stopped at 7-Eleven and bought an eighteen pack of beer. They sat on the stoop and drank beer. They shotgunned beers. They went into the backyard and lay in a hammock and smoked marijuana and talked. Abby said she was tired. Jordan said she could sleep in Daniel's bed probably. 'Let's go lie down,' Abby said. Jordan felt surprised that this was happening. He said okay. They lay in Daniel's bed. Abby guided Jordan's hand to her butt and he grabbed her butt. They kissed a little and Abby put her hand down Jordan's pants then took her hand out of Jordan's pants. They fell asleep.

*

'So, last night was fun,' Abby said the next morning. They were drinking coffee outside a coffee shop in Five Points. Ethan was inside buying food.

'Yeah,' Jordan said.

'We got like, weirdly handsy in bed and we should just talk about it because I feel like it's awkward,' Abby said and laughed a little. 'I think we should just talk about it.'

'Yeah. That was weird.'

'Yeah that was weird. How'd that happen?'

'I don't know. We got drunk and stoned.'

'It's okay,' Abby said. 'Don't stress out about it.'

'It's a little weird.'

'It's a little weird, but it's like not a big deal. Don't feel weird around me. It's cool.'

'Cool.'

'I was like, definitely a participant in that weird hand situation that occurred,' Abby said and laughed.

'Yeah.'

'Yeah, but we didn't do anything weird right? No. That could have been a lot weirder.'

'That could have been bad.'

'It was more like, kind of sad, honestly,' Abby said.

'It was like, drunk fumbling,' Jordan said.

'It's okay. Don't worry. It's only a little weird,' she said and laughed. 'That was so funny. It's alright. Was it weird? I don't know.'

'It was fine,' Jordan said.

'Can I have a sip of your coffee?' Abby said and drank coffee. 'That's delicious. That is fucking good. Oh no. Uh, that was so funny. How'd that happen? I don't understand. Let's just talk about it a little more. I feel like the more we talk about it the less like, weird it will be, but it's not weird.'

'Yeah, I don't know. I don't know.'

'What were we doing? I have no idea what that was.'

'It was just like, I don't know. Like a lot of arm touching, right?'

'Sure.'

'Just like, arm tickles.'

'Let's not do that again, maybe.'

'Yeah,' Jordan said. 'It didn't seem weird at the time.'

'It didn't. It really didn't, and then I woke up this morning and I was like that was a little weird.'

'It seemed good,' Jordan said. 'I had a good night. It was fun.'

'Me too. I'm just gonna keep going with it—' Ethan walked outside. 'Uh, never mind.'

*

Back at the house Ethan said he had to shower before work. 'Alright, take a shower,' Jordan said. He wanted to talk to Abby more.

Jordan and Abby sat on the couch, staring in different directions. Abby looked at Jordan, and said, 'I don't know why you guys bought a clear shower curtain. It's so weird. What if you have to go the bathroom?'

'Me and Ethan are very comfortable,' Jordan said in a mock-serious voice.

'So you watch each other shower?'

'Maybe.'

'Fuckin weird.'

'I just pee outside when he's in the shower.'

'I guess. I feel like I have to pee now…What are you doing today, Jordan?'

'Nothing.'

'I think it's gonna rain soon.'

Jordan stared at the coffee table, then glanced at Abby, who was looking at Jordan.

'We should probably talk more, shouldn't we?' Jordan said, suddenly feeling confident and articulate.

'Oh,' Abby said, in a slightly higher pitch than usual. Jordan thought she seemed interested in talking more. 'Do you wanna talk more?' she said.

'Yeah,' Jordan said

'Okay, what do you wanna talk about?'

'I don't know...I feel like I wasn't just drunk and horny,' Jordan said. 'I kind of like you, but I know you're like, with Natalie, and like—' He felt like he hinted at wanting to date Abby, which he hadn't really thought about before, because he thought she was a lesbian, but wasn't sure anymore. After she broke up with Daniel she told Daniel she was a lesbian and started talking to this girl named Natalie.

'Do you have a friend crush on me?' Abby said.

'Yeah, but like, I love you as friend and everything. I just didn't want you to think I was just, like, drunk and horny...I don't do things like that.'

'I think we just have a friend crush on each other,' Abby said.

'Me too,' Jordan said.

*

Jordan and Abby walked outside and sat on lawn chairs. Jordan picked up a beer can. 'Is this a full PBR? Did we kill that whole 18 pack?'

'No...that's not...possible.'

'I can't believe these chairs haven't broken yet. They always break.'

'They seem solid.'

'They break when my dad sits on them. He's a large man.'

'Can we still like, hangout and stuff?'

'What?' Jordan said.

'Can we still hangout?'

'Yes please,' Jordan said. 'I don't think it'll be weird. It won't be weird.'

'Cool,' Abby said. 'I don't think it's weird.'

'I don't either.'

'Yeah. It's not weird unless we make it weird. I don't think it's weird.'

'I just felt like I sounded like an asshole outside the coffee shop,' Jordan said.

'No. No. Not at all.'

Jordan stared at a small lizard walking slowly toward the can of beer. Abby looked at Jordan, then looked where Jordan was looking, at the lizard.

'He wants that beer,' Abby said.

'He wants that Pabst.'

'Where's PBR from?' Abby said.

'I think Missouri.'

'Milwaukee,' Abby said, staring at the can.

'Milwaukee...fuck yeah. We should move to Milwaukee.'

'No we shouldn't.'

'We could work for Pabst.'

'We could do that.'

'I could brew some PBR,' Jordan said.

'Established in Milwaukee,' Abby said, still staring at the can.

'Just like, brew PBR and think about all the people that are going to drink it later.'

'That's depressing.'

'I feel like, I'd be doing like, a good service to mankind.'

'I was at the car place to pick up my license the other day, and I had to fucking drive, like, twenty-five hours, and this random guy that worked there was so nice. He was like, let me like, put it on for you, and we were talking or whatever and he asked where I was from, and I was like, well, I was born in Chicago, and he was like, I knew I liked you. I'm from Milwaukee.'

'Shit...Did we shotgun one or two?'

'One. I think I wanted to do another one and you said no.'

'Yeah. I said I was gonna fall asleep on the floor.'

Abby laughed. 'It's nice out here. I just wanna lay in the sun all day with you.'

*

'I can't believe you've never been here,' Abby said to Jordan a few days later. 'It's like, really nice.' They were at Little Talbot Island, walking down a shady path toward the beach.

'Yeah. I've wanted to go here forever...I've been to that beach...or it was like, an island in Georgia with wild horses.'

'Cumberland?' Abby said.

'Yeah. That place is awesome.'

'I wanna go there...I think we're actually close to it.'

'I don't think it's that far.'

'Did you see a lot of wild horses?'

'Like, a dozen, maybe.'

'They just...run around?'

'Yeah,' Jordan said.

Abby looked at the swim trunks in Jordan's hand. 'How are you going to put those on?'

'Just, like, behind a tree.'

'Just wrap a towel around.'

'There's probably a restroom or something, maybe.'

'I don't think so,' Abby said.

'I can't believe I fell asleep on all that Adderall,' Jordan said. 'I took it at like ten thirty.' Jordan and Abby had hung out the night before. They slept in Daniel's bed together.

'I was exhausted last night...it was the red

wine...why did we open that bottle?' Abby said.

'Because we have a problem.'

'We were like, *we didn't get enough beer.*'

'We drank so much so fast,' Jordan said.

'That was fun though,' Abby said. 'I was like, shit-faced.'

'Oh yeah,' Jordan said. 'Yeah...I was fucked...not as fucked as I would have been without Adderall. I would have passed out in like an hour.'

'You think we're close, right?' Abby said.

'I think so,' Jordan said.

'Should we jog there?'

'Sure...Are you gonna have a heart attack?'

'That's not nice,' Abby said. 'Don't make fun of me.'

'I'm not,' Jordan said. 'Ready?'

'Yeah...but we also have to think we have not a lot of water.'

'We're gonna die out here,' Jordan said, jogging slowly.

They jogged for about two minutes, then Jordan noticed Abby breathing heavily. 'Okay, let's stop,' he said.

Abby handed Jordan a bottle of water. 'Thank you,' Jordan said. 'You never want to drink water when you're drunk.'

'Why would I?'

'Huh?'

'Why would I?'

'It makes you feel better in the morning.'

'I just like, reach next to my nightstand in the morning and chug a bottle of water and it feels so good...I should have peed when I had the chance...Whoa, dude...this is a long trail.'

'We're almost there.'

'I dunno.'

'On the map it says it's not far…Oh, it's right there, dude…Fuck yeah,' Jordan said as he and Abby approached an opening in the trees. They stood near the edge of a four or five foot drop-off that opened up to a white sand beach covered in driftwood.

'We just have to get down somehow.'

'Right here,' Jordan said. He pointed at a fairly steep, but walkable decline.

'I just like, can't believe places like this exist sometimes.'

'I know. I just wanna be at places like this more often. That's a lot of fucking driftwood.'

'I know. Where should we go?'

'I gotta change somewhere.'

'How did this happen?' Abby said, gesturing toward all the driftwood.

'I don't know…This is fucking awesome.'

'I'm gonna go in the water.'

'Oh, I can change in the water.'

'How?'

'I'm gonna put the towel over here.'

Jordan and Abby went in the water. Jordan took his shorts off and put his swimsuit on. They swam in the Intercoastal. They made fun of a family that was catching crabs. They got out of the water and laid on towels on the beach. An hour later they headed back to Abby's car.

'How much did we hike when we went on that trip in Georgia? How many miles was that?'

'I think it was like, seven…that's far.'

'It was pretty.'

'I thought we were gonna run out of water and then Daniel was gonna be like, *fuck you guys*.'

'Who do you think would have started eating people first?'

'Really?'

'Yeah, true.'

'He probably would have eaten Chelsea's dog.'

'Oh my God...I couldn't kill Myra...Yeah, Daniel would have been like, *you guys weren't aware of this, but I've been carrying a gun this whole time,* and that would have been it...one time we went to the movies and he took the gun from the side of his car door and like, put it in the back of his jeans and like, walked into the movies with it.'

'Fuck,' Jordan said.

'He was like, reaching, because he keeps a gun in his car, and he was like, reaching, and then went like this,' Abby said, and made a hand motion like she was putting something in the back of her pants. 'And I was like, *what'd you just put there*, and he was like, *my gun*. And I was like, *why the fuck do you need that? It's freaking me out*...and he was like, *you know, people shoot up movies*...and I'm like, *you're the shooter*...uh oh...Do you think he's gonna kill you when he gets home?'

'Probably.'

'No, Jordan—.'

'It's okay if he does.'

'He's not going to.'

'Sartre says you have to risk your life to know what it's worth.'

'He's not gonna kill you...we just have to like, clean up his room really well—'

'Yeah.'

'—I'm trying to think if I remember how everything was...like, before we started living in it.'

'I don't really remember...this last week has been

106

kind of a blur.'

'Uh oh…we just like, started living in his room…he like, left, and we were like, *well, this is our room now.*'

'Your ex-boyfriend's bed is really comfortable,' Jordan said and laughed. 'We kissed a lot last night.'

'A lot?'

'Yeah…for like, a long time.'

'We can't do that anymore,' Abby said.

'We said that last time.'

'I know…but what did we do about it?'

'We did it more,' Jordan said, and they both laughed.

'What do we do about it?'

'I don't know…what do you wanna do?'

'I don't know…what do you wanna do?'

'I don't know. I like it,' Jordan said. 'But, whatever you wanna do.'

'Jordan…we can't.'

'Alright,' he said.

'We have to be like, friends forever.'

'We will be.'

'I know,' Abby said. 'That's not good for friendships, right? That's not healthy.'

'Yeah. You're probably right.'

'I mean, I like it too, honestly, but —'

'Want some water?' Jordan said.

'Yeah.'

Jordan handed Abby water. 'Thank you.'

'You're welcome.'

'It smells good.'

'The water?'

'It smells like you.'

'Huh?'

'Smell it.'

Jordan smelled the bottle of water. 'That smells like

me?' he said.

'Yeah...that was like, a psycho-ass comment I just said.'

'That does smell good...why does this water bottle smell so good?'

'I don't know,' Abby said. 'Let me smell it.'

Jordan read the label. 'Oh, it's recycled plastic...that means it's, um, dirty plastic...I think.'

'It smells good,' Abby said. 'We kissed a lot last night.'

'Yeah we did.'

'Yeah...it was good though.'

'Yeah, I liked it,' Jordan said.

'I was like, trying to have sex with you last night.'

'And I was like, *you're too drunk. Let's have sex in the morning if you still want to.*'

'I remember...that would have been fucked up if you had sex with me...I was drunk.'

'Yeah. That's why I didn't do it.'

'That happens though. Like, that happens a lot.'

'Yeah.'

'How are we not gonna do that anymore? Just like, have self-control?'

'Yeah,' Jordan said. 'Yeah. We can do that. We can have self-control.'

*

'Jordan,' Eric texted Jordan around 10:30 a.m. a few days later.

'What's up?'

'JORDAN.'

'What? Are you Okay?'

'Yeah.'

'I'm reading about colonialism before noon,' Jordan said. 'I'm about to go make money for a white man that feeds chicken tenders to cops in his office.'

'Fucked.'

'A food runner.'

'I'm reading about institutional racism on the floor,' Eric said. 'A food runner.' Jordan got Eric a job as a food runner at the restaurant he worked at.

'Two food runners,' Jordan texted. 'We shouldn't define ourselves as food runners. Sartre says that's bad faith.'

'Sartre is my baby daddy. I'm drinking beer at 10:30 a.m. I am going to die. Things are fine. Things are fucked. All cops are bastards. Kill every cop you ever meet. Title of my memoir: I'm fucked/that's a spicy meatball.'

'Tony Hawk,' Jordan texted. 'Just think about Tony Hawk.'

'When I first read about the cop shootings I imagined the sniper saying to himself after every hit, *that's a spicy meatball.*' Someone had shot and killed a few cops the other day.

'Revolution News on Facebook makes me feel good.'

'That's not a spicy meatball.'

'The NSA is confused by our text messages. What is *Tony Hawk* code for, they wonder.'

'They know we are just dying.'

'We aren't a threat to anything but ourselves.'

'SERIN GAS DEPLOYED INTO THE BANK OF AMERICA BUILDING. WE DID IT. WE DID IT.'

'Are you on Revolution News?'

'Sorry just keeping them on their toes.'

'Dick Cheney just pooped.'

'Tony Hawk and Jeb Bush: the secret celebrity couple

everyone is talking about.'

'Washington Post finally stepping it up.'

'Five beers before noon,' Eric texted. 'I'm dead.'

'Once TPP passes we're all dead.'

'HOW? WHAT? I WAS IN THE MIDDLE OF TEXTING YOU THAT SENTENCE.'

'You're lying.'

'I was texting you about TPP and it was about us dying but also Arnold Schwarzenegger was involved. I'm watching a man at Walmart aggressively fan a crying infant with an unopened box of generic corn flakes.'

'He should bash the infant to death with generic corn flakes,' Jordan texted. He was in his car now, about to drive to work. 'My car smells like beer because it's covered in beer.'

'Tell Abby to stop covering your poor Honda in beer.'

Eric sent Jordan a screenshot of a message he sent to Kim, who works at Petco, that said, 'Hold a guinea pig and stroke the poor boy as you say, *there is no ecological future for any of you. The world cannot support your gaping mouths. The next world war will be over gasoline and water.*' He texted Jordan, 'These are things I say to a girl that really loves me. I'm fucked.'

'Stroke the poor boy. Jesus.'

'She is teaching kids about ocean life, and this is what I say to her. I'm drunk and on Adderall. If they try to call me in today tell them I'm indisposed. Today is rock bottom and I'm okay with it. I said to Kim, *tell them about pipelines and Dick Cheney. We are the apex predator of the goddamn universe.* I love this girl. The world is literally falling apart. We are coming undone as a species. Living between world wars forever. And

Donald Trump is going to be president, probably.'

At work about thirty minutes later Jordan texted Eric, 'Expediting on Adderall. No thrill quite like it. Singing Pat the Bunny in my head. My life seems absurd right now.'

'It is.'

'It's nice to be young.'

'I don't wanna get old.'

'Me neither. I'm glad I'm not really ugly or blind or something else shitty.'

Jordan sent Eric a picture of him and Abby in the kitchen, eating PB&J tacos, surrounded by empty beer cans. He texted, 'I feel like this picture sums up my life well.'

'You are taco man and Abby is sin glasses.'

*

Around dusk the next day, after stopping at the Fresh Market to pick up a twelve pack of beer, Jordan drove to a gated community near the beach to see Abby. She was watching her cousin's mansion while her and her husband were in Paris.

'I kind of want to do mushrooms,' Jordan said to Abby while lying next to her on a cushiony lounge chair by the pool, after each drinking four or five beers. Jordan had bought some mushrooms and some LSD the other day.

'Should we?' Abby said.

'Yeah.'

'Let's just look at them.'

He walked outside the mansion then out through the front door to his car and removed a small bag of mushrooms from his secret compartment next to his backseat. 'I'm going to eat one,' he said outside, and did, then asked Abby if she wanted one also. Abby said she was going to wait twenty minutes to see how Jordan was feeling. She Googled 'mushrooms adderall alcohol' on her phone.

'What does the internet say?'

'That it's a bad idea.'

'Hmm,' Jordan said.

They both read about mixing drugs on forums for about five minutes, then, after agreeing that mixing the three drugs would probably feel normal, because they already mix amphetamines and alcohol frequently and have probably built up a tolerance, they both ingested two large mushrooms. Jordan stared at the bag, which contained three mushrooms, and said, 'We should just do the rest of them,' then ate two medium-sized mushrooms and Abby ate one large-sized mushroom.

*

While sitting in the hot tub with Abby, waiting for the mushrooms to start working, Jordan heard four knocks at the door. A few seconds later, after discerning the noise, Jordan felt briefly frightened, then, after thinking it seemed sitcom-like that an unknown person would unexpectedly knock on the door of a house he wasn't supposed to be in, ten minutes after ingesting mushrooms (currently a schedule one drug in the U.S., along with heroin, LSD, marijuana, mescaline, MDMA, GHB, and ecstasy) he felt amused, and convinced himself — as a means of delaying accepting the potential seriousness of the situation, maybe — that he would have an awkwardly funny interaction with whoever was at the door. Then he remembered that he wasn't in a sitcom and felt frightened. Abby made a face at Jordan. She stood slowly and walked toward the sliding glass door, then peered through the glass, and looked at the front door, which had a decently-sized, semi-transparent glass window. 'Holy shit,' she said. 'It's my mom.'

'Fuck,' Jordan said. 'Wait, no. It's okay. We just took them. We can do this.'

'Are there shrooms on the counter?' Abby said.

'No. I don't think so. I'll hide the baggy though.'

Jordan jogged inside the mansion and put the baggy underneath Abby's bathing suit. He walked outside and lay on a lounge chair for about three seconds, then nervously stood and walked toward the back door. He heard Abby and her mom talking about Bonefish Grill — where her mom, Abby explained earlier, had gone on a Match.com date — and felt relieved because her mom seemed drunk, but then thought, feeling mildly, but controllably self-conscious about being on mushrooms, that maybe she only seemed drunk because he was on mushrooms.

Jordan introduced himself to Abby's mom. She talked about Bonefish grill more. 'The Bang Bang Shrimp is really good there,' Jordan said. He felt surprised that he was able to enter the conversation so quickly. After about five minutes of what seemed to Jordan like a normal conversation, Abby's mom started telling a story about how she matched with one of her friend's ex-husbands, or something.

'I can't deal with this story right now,' Abby said frantically.

'It's not that weird,' Abby's mom said.

'I can't deal with this,' Abby said. 'Like, at all.'

'Okay,' Abby's mom said. No one said anything for a second. 'I'll go ahead and leave you guys alone.'

*

'That went okay, right?' Jordan said, smiling.

'Yeah. I think it was fine. I started feeling the mushrooms when she started talking about Match.com. I just kept thinking about the internet. About online dating, and didn't like it.'

'That could have been bad. I'm glad she didn't show up like, an hour from now.'

'Should we jump in the pool?'

'Yeah,' Jordan said and they both jumped in the pool.

Jordan saw a large green ball floating in the pool.

'Look at this ball,' Jordan said.

'It's beautiful,' Abby said.

*

Abby and Jordan walked down a narrow brick path toward the pier. The house was on the Intercoastal Waterway. They sat down on a pool towel and looked up at the stars.

'Is that a star or a plane?' Abby said.

'I think that's a plane,' Jordan said.

'Where do you think it's going?'

'Alaska.'

'It seems like, um, it's going to Hawaii. It would need a layover for Alaska...I guess it would need one for Hawaii, too.'

They looked at two planes that seemed to be flying directly toward each other.

'There's too many planes up there,' Abby said.

'I think they have like, a lot of space.'

'That plane just hit a star and it didn't even know.'

'That plane is an idiot,' Jordan said.

Abby pointed at another plane. 'This one is going to Alabama. Definitely.'

'Fuck everyone on that plane,' Jordan said, and laughed.

Abby pointed at another plane. 'This one is going to New York.' She asked Jordan if he believed in aliens.

'Um, I think so. I don't ever really think about aliens.'

'I think they exist when I'm sober, but right now I feel like, maybe this is all there is. Maybe this is it. People just want more. They want an explanation for everything, but maybe this is just it. Yeah,' Abby said, sounding self-assured. 'This is it.'

'I like that a lot,' Jordan said. 'I feel like thinking, *this is it*, is the best thought to have while on mushrooms. I don't care about aliens.'

'People on the internet are stupid. Adderall and mushrooms are so nice. Like, really just so nice.'

'People on the internet don't know anything,' Jordan said. 'I can't believe there's an American flag on the fucking moon. I can't even think about that. When I'm on mushrooms I care about all living things more and I dislike money even more than usual. These stars are so nice.'

'They're, like, so nice. This house is too big. I made peace with it though when I went to the restroom. And I looked at myself in the mirror. I thought, *this is what I am. Whatever I am. And that's okay*.'

'I kept thinking, *this is me*. And felt glad that I'm in shape again. I kept opening and closing my mouth a lot.'

'When I looked in the mirror while on MDMA I felt really beautiful. I don't like the way I look when I'm drunk though. I think you would enjoy MDMA. We should do some.'

'Yeah. Okay.'

'This is so nice.'

'I think, so far, this is one of my favorite drug experiences. I feel like everyone should take mushrooms.'

'I feel like my face is stuck in a smile for no reason. It just feels natural to smile.'

Jordan felt the complete opposite of how he felt while on LSD with Chelsea. He was glad he didn't feel like ignoring Abby while on mushrooms. He also felt glad that Abby wasn't ignoring him either, and that they were both having similar experiences, it seemed, based on their conversation.

'It feels nice not to have anything that I feel like I need to figure out right now,' Jordan said.

'That's good,' Abby said. 'I feel happy. When you took acid I felt like you were just in your head a lot, and you actually figured things out, and acted on them, and they were good decisions, I think. I can definitely see how you could be depressed and take mushrooms and figure out your life though. I think I just realize that so many things that, uh, we're taught to care about, are just like, bullshit. Do you still like me after doing drugs with me?'

'Yeah. I like you a lot.'

'I like you a lot.'

*

Jordan and Abby woke up around noon the next morning. They each took an Adderall and cleaned the house. They went outside and sat on lounge chairs. Jordan read *The Sixth Extinction* by Elizabeth Kolbert and Abby read *Best Behavior* by Noah Cicero. An hour later they drove Abby's car to UNF to pick up Jordan's cap and gown and graduation tickets. They drove to the Fresh Market and bought salmon, hummus, cucumbers, green peppers, corn, red onions, lettuce, and a twelve pack of beer, then went back to the house and ate salads. They sat in the pool and drank beer and watched the rain. They split an Adderall. They sat in the hot tub and kissed. They listened to *The Life of Pablo* by Kanye West and drank the twelve pack of beer, then a bottle of wine. They moved to the outside couch and had sex then went inside, on the bed, and had sex. They got in the bathtub and cleaned each other. Jordan went into the kitchen and got a banana and they shared the banana. Jordan cut his leg on the edge of the hot tub, and Abby got a towel and cleaned up the blood. Jordan was graduating from college the next morning.

*

Jordan woke at 7:30 a.m. and took an Adderall, then drove to UNF. He sat alone in a long white hallway in the auditorium. He was wearing a gown. About ten minutes later Jordan saw Chelsea walking down the hallway. 'Fuck,' he thought. She sat next to Jordan.

'I wonder how long this is supposed to last,' Jordan said.

'I don't know. We showed up way too early. When'd you get here?'

'Probably just like, fifteen minutes ago.'

The hallway started filling up with people in gowns. Jordan's friend, Shithead, came and stood next to Jordan. Jordan had texted Shithead about how he was seeing Abby the other night.

'So who's this girl you've been seeing? Abby, right?'

Jordan shook his head and made a noise like he wanted Shithead to stop talking.

Jordan heard Chelsea start crying a little.

*

Later that night Jordan read *The Shock Doctrine* by Naomi Klein on a lounge chair in the sunlight by the pool. Abby opened the back door around 2 p.m. after returning from work and suggested, after a few minutes of casual conversation, that they each take an Adderall and read for a while. They each took an Adderall. Abby read a biography about John Brown, which Jordan had suggested and let her borrow, and he continued reading *The Shock Doctrine*, then finished a chapter about South Africa and said, 'It's nice out. We should take Acid.'

'Okay,' Abby said, seeming less hesitant than when Jordan suggested doing mushrooms, and they each ingested one strip of acid, then walked to the dock, laid down on a pool towel, and waited for the drugs to start working.

*

'Kanye West and trees are the only things that exist right now,' Abby said while lying on a lounge chair next to Jordan, shortly after leaving the dock in a hurry, because the clouds, Abby had frantically said, looked like 'the cat from Alice in Wonderland,' and were scaring her. Jordan thought, feeling mildly anxious about the downward-seeming trajectory of Abby's acid trip so far, 'Abby wants to be alone on the chair,' and mumbled, 'I'm going in the pool,' then slowly and cautiously entered the pool, unsure of what the water would feel like, and swam around the edge of the rectangular pool about four times, uncomfortably feeling like he was swimming through jello, then went and sat on a slightly submerged, seat-like ledge near the deep-end. He stared at the house, which looked shadowy and medieval, and felt overwhelmed by the uncountable-seeming number of protruding angles, and stared at a large oak tree and listened intently to Kanye West, currently a lyric-less computer-y beat, self-consciously trying not to think about anything, and thought, 'not thinking about anything,' repetitively, for a minute, gradually becoming less aware of his surroundings, then, after gradually becoming aware that he wasn't aware of his surroundings, became aware again, and weakly discerned Abby's voice, which Jordan thought seemed mildly softer than usual, and heard her say, 'I feel like this pool chair is the only safe place,' and Jordan intuitively and silently agreed.

*

'I don't like acid,' Abby said inside the house about thirty minutes later.

Jordan was trying to make salad and couscous. 'I don't think I do either,' he said. 'I don't want to be on a drug where I'm not capable of making a salad.'

'People that take acid frequently probably hate reality. It's just like, so unlike reality. I think I just like my life right now.'

'I'm happy with everything. Yeah. I like my life. I don't like acid,' Jordan said and waved a knife through the air. 'I feel like I'm like, ironically on acid. Acid is dumb. It's just a dumb drug. What am I doing right now? What is this knife for?' he said and laughed.

'I thought you were making couscous?' Abby said. 'Do you remember?'

'Remember?'

'How to make couscous?'

'Yeah…I think so. I just have to get the water to like, boil. Yeah. I can make couscous. I'm capable.'

*

They ate couscous and salad. 'I know what we should do,' Abby said enthusiastically. She smiled.

'What?' Jordan said, smiling.

'The grass,' Abby said, and stood suddenly, walked outside, grabbed a beach towel off the lounge chair, then held Jordan's hand and lead him outside the screened-in pool deck.

'I felt like the screen was closing in a little…maybe not, like, closing in, but it felt very tight, like the area seemed so small.'

'Nothing seems okay right now,' Abby said while staring at the sky. 'I can't look at the house. I just like the trees, I think, because everything else seems awful.'

'It's because we're on drugs, I think,' Jordan said. 'We took acid.'

'I forgot we were on drugs,' Abby said. 'We're on drugs,' she said loudly, then made a noise like she was relieved.

'We're on drugs,' Jordan said and laughed. 'Maybe we shouldn't yell about being on drugs so much though. I think that's why acid makes people freak out. They like, forget that they took drugs, and mistake whatever is happening for reality. I'm usually good at taking drugs and thinking *I'm on drugs*, and not freaking out.'

'I'm glad we only took one strip. I couldn't look at

your face, Jordan. It was so long. I couldn't even kiss you.'

'That's okay —'

'I like, love your face. The acid was just making me not love your face. I mean, I'm still definitely on acid, but I like your face again.'

*

In bed an hour later Abby stared at the chandelier with amazement, and said that she was still tripping, and kissed Jordan on the neck. 'I feel like I'm kissing a baby dolphin,' she said.

'Do you have a thing for baby dolphins?' Jordan said.

'I do now,' Abby said, and smiled endearingly. Jordan felt relieved that Abby could look at his face and kiss him again.

*

On Monday, August 15, 2016, around 2 a.m. Jordan and Abby had sex in his bed. 'Do you wanna be my girlfriend?' he said after.

'Yeah,' Abby said. 'Do you wanna be my boyfriend?'

Jordan said that he did. They lied in bed and kissed and looked at each other. Jordan said he had to pee and walked outside the bedroom, wearing only boxers. He heard the front door knob turn and saw the door open and then saw Daniel standing in the doorway.

'Uh, hey man,' Jordan said.

'What's up?' Daniel said. He gave Jordan a hug. Jordan saw Abby's purse on the coffee table while looking over Daniel's shoulder.

'I've gotta pee,' Jordan said. He walked into the

bathroom and locked the door. He sat on the floor against the door and tried to think. He was a little drunk. He sat and thought things like, 'Daniel is going to fucking shoot me' and 'I'm about to fucking die.' He took his boxers off without thinking and got in the shower. Ethan was home, too. Jordan thought Ethan would handle the situation and make Daniel leave so that he didn't kill him and Abby.

Daniel knocked on the door. 'Hey man, come out,' he said. 'Let's talk.'

'I'm in the shower,' Jordan yelled.

A few minutes later Daniel pounded on the door. Jordan turned off the water and dried off and put his clothes back on. He opened the door. Daniel was standing there, smiling. He grabbed Jordan by the shoulder. 'I'm gonna kill you,' he said, then laughed. 'Just kidding.' He told Jordan to come sit on the porch with him so they could talk 'man to man.'

*

About thirty minutes later Jordan and Abby got in Abby's car to drive to her dad's house to sleep. 'He picked me up like baby Jesus, naked, out of your bed. Please, God. Fuck,' she said. 'I left my phone. I can't leave Ethan there.'

'Ethan will be fine,' Jordan said.

'I don't trust it,' Abby said. 'Daniel picked me up like goddamn baby Jesus, naked. I thought it was a goddamn dream, because I was passed out until I realized, this is not a dream, and opened my eyes for twenty seconds, and was like, *I am fucked. Get me out of your arms.* I was like, *please let me down, please let me down.* And he was like, *Abby, calm down, calm down,* and I was like, *I'm naked, put me down, put me down.* It was scary.'

'What did he say?' Jordan said.

'He said nothing,' Abby said.

'What did he say after you said, *put me down*?'

'He waited a little while and was like, *Abby it's okay*, and I was like, *please put me down.*'

'That was insanity,' Jordan said.

'I didn't think that was gonna happen.'

'I didn't think he was gonna let me leave the house,' Jordan said.

'I'm scared, I'm scared for Ethan, I don't want him to die,' Abby said.

'He's not gonna hurt Ethan, dude. He's fine. Like, he's fine.'

'Is he gonna come to my house?'

'If he's gonna hurt anyone it would be us. He apologized for sleeping in your driveway.' One time after they broke up Daniel got drunk and drove to Abby's house and slept in her driveway. 'He's fine. He's not that insane. He really isn't. Holy fuck. I was in the shower just doing this for like, thirty minutes,' he said, while running his hands through his hair, 'just being like, *fuck fuck fuck fuck fuck* —'

'I was like, *Jordan ran out the window*. I was like, *Jordan Jordan.*'

'No...I was like, *Ethan's gonna get him out of* —'

'Ethan's so smooth.'

' *— the fucking house tonight.*'

'And I was like, by myself, and I was like, *Jordan Jordan Jordan,* and I was like, *Jordan left* —'

Abby pulled into the corner store parking lot. 'What are you getting?' Jordan said.

'Cigarettes.'

'Okay.'

'And I was like, *Jordan left, Jordan left us* —'

'No I was just in the fucking shower for some reason, like it's a good idea to take a shower right now.'

'Ugh, I'm gonna kill myself,' Abby said, and opened the door, stepped out of the car.

'No, we're fine,' Jordan said, and watched Abby walk inside the gas station. Jordan turned on the radio. Jazz was playing on NPR. He felt relieved that Daniel knew he was dating Abby, and that he didn't get shot in the head.

A few minutes later Abby got back in the car. She said, 'Jordan, what'd you tell him?'

'Tell Ethan?'

'What'd you tell Daniel? Everything? You told him everything?' she said.

'Yeah I did. We sat on the porch and I told him everything, and he's fine. Can you tell me where to go?'

'Yes.'

'I did. He knows it. He knows everything now.'

'You have diarrhea of the mouth.'

'What was I gonna do? At that point there's no denying anything.'

'Turn on Beaver Street.'

'Take a right here?'

'I'm gonna throw up...he just picked my naked body up out of your bed —'

'That's bizarre.'

'It was disgusting. I thought it was a nightmare until I realized it was not a goddamn drill.'

'Jesus fuck.'

'My thoughts exactly. Oh my God.'

'I said, *I thought you were gonna shoot me in the head, man.* He said, *no, it's fine, she's really hot*...and I was like...*are you being...what the fuck are you doing dude, like, what the fuck is your deal —'*

'Jordan, he picked my naked body up.'

'That's fucking bizarre.'

'It's disgusting…I feel very violated.'

'I'm not going back there ever again…where do I go?'

'Straight. Arlington Expressway.'

'Holy fuck.'

'Oh my fuck.'

'That was the most stressful situation of my entire life —'

'I thought it was a nightmare…I was like, fuck —'

'I'm so glad I'm not there anymore.'

'I'm gonna throw up. Ethan's still there.'

'Ethan's fine. He didn't do anything wrong.'

'I need to rescue him. I don't like that he's there, dude. I need to know what's going on —'

'Where do I go?'

'Straight.'

'He was like, *I don't care, but I gotta warn you about her*, and I was like, *dude you're just fucking being a jealous asshole, sorry.*'

'Warn you about what?'

'Um, just fucking being weird. He was being so goddamn weird, like —'

'Jordan —'

'—that's the first thing you say after you find out your roommate is dating your ex-girlfriend? Isn't she hot? What the fuck? What the fuck?'

'Dude —'

'That's insane.'

'—he picked my naked body up.'

'That's insane.'

'That is insane…I was like, *is this a nightmare?* And

then I was like, *this is not a nightmare*. I was passed out—'

'Holy fuck.'

'—I was literally passed out…passed out…I thought it was a nightmare…and then I opened my eyes again and I was like, *oh my God, no*…I was like, *please put me down, please put me down,* and then he finally put me down.'

'This way?'

'Yes…that was Chernobyl. That was Chernobyl—

'That was bad.'

'I wanna die.'

'Oh my God.'

'I don't like it. I don't like it. I can't—'

'What?'

'I can't believe Ethan's in the house.'

'Ethan is fine,' Jordan said.

'Ethan was so normal—'

'So was—'

'—How'd he do it?'

'Daniel was being Daniel but he wasn't hitting me in the face.'

'He didn't pull a gun.'

'He didn't shoot me in the head. He didn't hit me. Holy shit.'

'Uh, how is this real? Jordan, I hope he doesn't come to my house.'

'Huh?'

'I hope he doesn't come to my house.'

'He's not going to.'

'You don't think?'

'No…I know he's not.'

'Should I call Ethan?'

'No…let's wait 'til we get to your place.'

'Okay. I need to call Ethan.'

'Oh fuck.'

'Oh fuck.'

'He was knocking on the bathroom door, and I was just like, *I'm peeing, I'm peeing*...holy fuck.'

'Did he ask, or you just told?'

'I don't remember. Hold on. I gotta think. My head's fucking weird right now.'

'Alright...I love that I went into the gas station and the first thing...I walked in, and was like, *I need a Xanax*, and all the homeless men were like, *preach*.'

Jordan laughed.

'They were like, *heard that*,' Abby said. 'I was like, *please, someone give me drugs. I need crack. I need crack.* I never thought I wanted crack until now...I'll tell you when to turn...I hate my life. I hate my life —'

'Why?' Jordan said. 'We're good now. Like, the worst is over. That was as bad as it could have been.'

'No —'

'Wait, what do you mean?'

' —I did not think that would happen, dude.'

'I didn't either...I was not ready for him to come home —'

'Why didn't he say like, *hey, by the way, I'm coming home*? Fuck.'

'Thank God I was drunk. Holy fuck. I couldn't have dealt with that if I wasn't drunk.'

'What a psychopath...I need to drown myself in wine.'

'Thank God I was drunk. Holy shit.'

'Jordan, I'm traumatized.'

'That was traumatizing.'

'I'm traumatized. Dude —'

'Holy fuck.'

' —you did not get your naked body picked up.'

'No, you're right.'

'I was naked in bed and I got picked up.'

'Oh shit...I'm sorry he picked you up naked, that's...I'm sorry, that's terrible. That's—'

'Dude—'

'—Fucking awful.'

'—I thought I was in a goddamn nightmare.'

'So did I...but your nightmare was way worse than mine.'

'I got naked picked up.'

'Holy fuck.'

*

A couple weeks later Jordan stood in the ocean with only his head and neck above water. Abby was lying on a beach towel in a light blue swimsuit. Jordan watched her stand and run into the ocean. He swam toward the shore then stood with the upper half of his body exposed and hugged Abby, until a wave crashed on top of them. After emerging from the water, Jordan inhaled and heard thunder. He remembered that he and Abby had both eaten mushrooms about an hour earlier, in the parking lot of a Mexican restaurant, where he and Emma used to eat sometimes. Abby said they were going to get struck by lightning, then turned around, without waiting for a response from Jordan, and walked back toward the shore. They lay on a towel and listened to Frank Ocean's new album and held each other. They walked back to Abby's car and drove downtown. They went to a smoke-filled cigar bar and ordered Jamaican ginger beers, then sat outside in sunlight and shared a cigarette. Jordan saw a man in a Jack Daniels t-shirt holding hands with a woman in mom jeans and said that he thought they had good sex, and Abby agreed. They each drank two more beers then walked to Abby's car and each ate two more mushrooms. They walked across the street to Fort Matanzas—an old Spanish fort made of coquina. They walked along a narrow path along the water then sat and stared at the Intercoastal. They made fun of a couple that was getting professional pictures taken of themselves in different poses. Jordan suggested that they drive to Nobbies, a dive bar that sometimes had punk shows, and Abby said okay, and they drove to Nobbies. Jordan bought two beers and they sat outside Nobbies, facing the road, and drank beer and listened to the band Destroyer on Jordan's phone. Abby said they should follow Destroyer on tour and Jordan said that sounded like fun, and Googled 'Destroyer tour' and saw that they were playing a show in Austin, Texas, in November, and said that maybe they should go. Abby said that she's always wanted to go to Austin. Jordan said that there was a pier on the Intercoastal in the neighborhood next to his parent's neighborhood and that they could go there. Abby said that sounded good and that she was hungry. Jordan said they could get Hungry Howie's pizza and eat it at the pier, then remembered that there was a Little Caesars near his house and said that they could go there instead, if Abby wanted. Abby said she loved Little Caesars, and Jordan felt surprised, thinking that most people he knew didn't like Little Caesars. At the Little Caesars, which was inside a gas station, Jordan bought a cheese pizza while Abby grabbed a four pack of tallboys. After buying the pizza, Jordan walked toward Abby, who was standing in line with the beer, and thought (due to mushrooms) that most products in the gas station were extremely unhealthy, and seemed like things that were designed specifically to kill a person slowly. Inside the car, he felt surprised when he expressed concern that the world doesn't encourage people to develop. Abby said that college was good because you could escape working at Little Caesars, and Jordan thought about the student loan crisis, but didn't say anything. At the entrance to the pier Abby parked the car and told Jordan to get the mushrooms out of the glove box, and he did, and they ate four mushrooms each. They walked toward the end of the pier with the pizza, the beer, and a pillow. At the end of the pier they drank beer and ate pizza and listened to Destroyer. They lay down and held each other. A few minutes later it was raining. 'Put your head under the pillow,' Abby said, and they both put their heads under the pillow.

About the Author

Blake Middleton lives in Jacksonville, Florida. He tweets @blaketheidiot. He's on Instagram @middleton.blake.